THE MIDLIFE CANCER'S GUIDE TO A BAD HOROSCOPE

POWERS OF THE ZODIAC - BOOK THREE

KATE KARYUS QUINN   DEMITRIA LUNETTA
MARLEY LYNN

CONTENTS

PREFACE

Visit MarleyLynn.com to sign up for our Newsletter and you'll receive **FREE SHORT STORIES!**

Like us on Facebook to stay in touch, enter giveaways, and know when all our newest titles are about to drop!

PROLOGUE

shes to ashes. Dust to dust. Flesh to Hydra.

Okay, maybe that's not how the saying usually goes, but tonight is all about the unusual. And the plain old awful.

I came to this abandoned warehouse on the Jersey Shore armed for battle, ready to save my husband's life. Instead I ended up feeding his dead body to a Hydra, and meeting the two other women he's also apparently married to.

Helena, aka wife #2, said we don't have time to wait for Bobby's body to turn to dust. We had to dispose of him tonight.

It's a pretty cold way of talking about your husband whose body isn't even cold yet, but she's clearly the practical type. She's also a high-powered lawyer and when she says that no one will believe we didn't murder him after finding out the truth, it's easy to believe she knows what she's talking about.

Still, I would never have agreed to it if a part of me wasn't certain that Bobby would get a kick out of this method of... er...burial. He was big on wanting to be special and different from everyone else. And I think being eaten by the Jersey Shore Hydra definitely counts as unique.

That doesn't mean that it's easy to hear the monster chew up his corpse. The wet slurping sounds are horrible, but I try to think about the circle of life. I try to think about how happy Bobby made me, for a short while. I definitely try NOT to think about how I've gone from newlywed to widow over the course of my birthday weekend.

It's been a long day, and the chamomile crown I'm wearing has slipped to the side, dangling over one ear. When I say I came here armed for battle, what I mean is that Harmony—my mother—decked me out for mystical warfare. I'm covered in dragon's blood oil, wearing a pentagram charm, and have garlic bulbs hanging around my neck.

The two other women—who I now know are my sister wives—are nothing like me. They both stand, surveying the rippling water where the Hydra has taken Bobby's body. Maddie, Bobby's first wife and high school girlfriend, is wearing a white dress and sniffling. She was supposed to have a vow renewal ceremony with him today, on their twenty-fifth anniversary.

Helena is obviously another story. The waves of anger coming off her could warm a whole house on a cold winter evening. Helena isn't sad—she's pissed.

She's clearly not feeling a bond with me, or Maddie, the way I am. I have an inkling she'd be just as happy to toss the two of us in for the Hydra's dessert. I understand where she's coming from. I wasn't exactly thrilled to find out that I wasn't Bobby's one and only. But since that's not how it happened, I focus on the silver lining. And the one I find is nice and shiny. There are three of us...and three has always been my lucky number.

Not that I'm feeling lucky right now. But these things often take time.

"I need a minute," I say to them, adjusting my crown. Neither of the women pay me any mind, and I wander back to the warehouse on the wharf where everything went down. The *talentum dei*, a magical object that Bobby had discovered while operating his business as an artifacts dealer, still sits on a patch of concrete, looking all innocent —like it didn't just wreak some serious havoc.

The supernatural can be like that sometimes. Hiding in plain sight.

Years ago, humanity was suddenly—and forcefully—made aware that all the creatures we'd been told stories about for years; vampires, werewolves, harpies, hydras, mermaids, you name it—were actually quite real. The supernatural creatures had become part of our world, and magic wasn't just a fairy tale anymore.

Lots of people were surprised...and not in a good way. Harmony likes to say that it wasn't just the supes who made themselves known—the small-minded bigots did as well.

Others, like Bobby, saw it as an opportunity. With supes living and working side by side with humans, Bobby's job as an artifacts dealer specializing in magical objects became quite lucrative...but I doubt he expected it to end with him being digested by a water monster while his trio of wives looked on.

I walk over to the *talentum* and begin to dismantle it back into three parts. Bobby had given each of his wives a section for safekeeping, none of us knowing its true purpose. Maddie had a globe of the earth, while Helena had the base.

It turned out that the wedding present he'd given me, a giant gold ring, was the last piece to complete the trio. A gold ring might make sense for most women as a gift, but it wasn't the kind of ring you wear. It was at least a foot wide and had the twelve zodiac signs around the circle.

It was the perfect present for me. The perfect present, from my perfect husband.

The first thing most kids learn is their name, numbers, and the alphabet. Not me. Well, I did learn my name, but even more important than that—was my sign.

"You are a Cancer," Harmony told me from a very young age. "It's a water sign and some will say it's not powerful. Those people are wrong."

I never cared about being powerful...which is pretty typical for a water sign. We tend to be a gentle, dreamy type of people. I guess it was lucky that I am unlike my mother— who can read palms and sometimes even get a glimpse of the future. Small and often cryptic glimpses.

Sometimes she shares bits of them with me, but not often. Harmony says there's nothing more deadly than being told one's destiny.

"What about all the people who come to you and ask you to read their palms or tell their fortunes?" I used to ask.

"I never tell anyone anything that could compromise their destiny."

Despite all the people who call her a scam artist (her main business is reading palms and even in our newly enlightened age where everyone knows and accepts that supernatural creatures walk among us, there are still those who can't wrap their minds around my mother being able to know who they are just by looking at the lines in their hand), but Harmony is bound by a strict code of ethics that she wouldn't break for anyone.

Not even her only daughter. Even when it might've saved Bobby's life.

Unlike Harmony, I don't have any connection with the supernatural. I can't see glimpses of the future or read auras as easily as the newspaper.

I was just a normal woman.

But I think that I'm not anymore.

Which explains the prediction Harmony threw out right before I left the house tonight. She said, "He will be the making of you."

It was a surprising thing for her to say because she doesn't like Bobby at all and thinks I'm an idiot for marrying him.

Now, I understand why she changed her tune. She must've gotten a glimpse of what would happen with the *talentum*. Which means she probably also suspected—or outright knew—how Bobby would die. Or maybe not. Who can say. That's the thing about the future, it's a very topsy turvy thing.

Still, I can't help but feel a little resentful that she didn't give me a better warning. Even after discovering all of Bobby's lies, I still would've saved him if I could have.

I bend down and lift the ring off the other two pieces, setting each part a good distance from each other, just in case. What I had thought was just an interesting, zodiac-aligned ring of metal was actually an incredibly powerful object, called a *talentum dei*. Alone, it was powerless. Combined with the other two sections, it became quite deadly.

"I'm sorry, Bobby," I say, eyeing the spot where his body had lain.

But I can't mourn him too deeply—because he isn't the only person who died here tonight. My husband wasn't just a polygamist; he was also a con artist and his last mark had been his own wives.

All three of us had received panicked phone calls from him, insisting that we needed to bring our pieces of the *talentum* to this wharf to exchange for his life. He'd been kidnapped by people who wanted the *talentum* for themselves, powerful people who knew what the object could do— bestow the powers of a god onto a human being.

Bobby had orchestrated the whole thing. With the *talentum* assembled, Bobby murdered two people in cold blood. Well, maybe it was in hot blood. I don't like to be judgmental. And who can say if the kidnappers were bad guys or just desper- ate; we can never fully know someone else's journey. At the same time...they were also prepared to kill for the *talentum's* powers, which is not a very nice thing to do.

Bobby beat them to the punch, though. Or to the shot, I guess. He killed them and then used their blood as a sacrifice, smearing it on the *talentum* so that he could become a god. He knew it required the sacrifice of a human life, but it didn't work out the way Bobby had anticipated.

The three pieces of the *talentum dei* came together, throwing tentacles of magical power all over the place. Or, well, only in three places—me, Maddie, and Helena. Meanwhile Bobby had made his own dive for the *talentum*, only to have it fry him right there.

As I cradle my piece of the *talentum* close to my chest, I understand why it killed Bobby.

He wasn't worthy. Not even close.

Instead, it chose us, the wives.

The three of us were lifted into the air, surrounded by torrents of magic. Maddie was engulfed by a funnel of air, like a tornado, but it didn't hurt her at all. I could see she was terrified, and I'd wanted to tell her it was okay, that this was magic—real magic—and that fighting it was pointless.

I'm pretty sure all Helena knows is fighting. She was enveloped in earth, clods of dirt and dust circling around her, while she screamed what I'm pretty sure was all just a string of swear words and threats. I don't know who she thought she was swearing at, or what power she had in that moment, but I knew better. I knew what this was—I'd spent my whole life living in Harmony's household, a place where magic and reality blended long before the supes showed up in our world and proved to everyone that people like Harmony and I weren't crazy.

But still, I'd never had direct, physical experience with powerful forces like this, and even though I had no idea what was happening to me, I made a decision right here, to trust it. To go with it. I guess it's just my optimistic nature.

Being an optimist is not the same thing as being stupid, but you wouldn't guess it by the way people treat me. I was being optimistic when I got married for the very first time at the age of forty. I'd never wanted to marry anyone, but then I met Bobby.

He was so confident, so devoted, and downright sexy to boot. Sure, we'd only known each other for a few months. But I was being optimistic when I said yes, believing that good things come to those who wait. And I had waited. A very, very, long time. Most of the girls I'd graduated from high school with were on their second or third marriages, and doing a hard restart while asking their first batch of kids to help raise the second.

Me? I'd passed on love more than once, turned down some offers for my hand because Harmony took a glance at theirs and proclaimed them unworthy.

It wasn't dirt under their fingernails or the calluses of a blue-collar worker that turned Harmony off my former suitors. It was their life lines and love lines—or, as she once referred to it in the backroom after doing a reading for a client—their liar lines. Harmony could read fate in the palms of just about anyone, and right up until Bobby, no one had been good enough for me, her only child.

Not that she thought he was, either. According to her, he was the worst of the lot.

But that time I didn't listen, because I'm a glass-half-full kind of girl.

I dove right into that tall glass of water, flying to Vegas with Bobby for my birthday weekend. And when we said our vows in front of Elvis, I was more than just optimistic, I was overflowing with faith in my man. We celebrated in bed, where our bodies and souls became one. It was amazing and special and while some women might've been bothered by Bobby calling out the name of his dead wife (who I later found out wasn't so dead), I just knew I'd picked a man whose love went deep.

I was still holding on determinedly to that optimism when we landed back home in Jersey and he immediately split, telling me there was a work emergency...which seemed odd because he was an antiques dealer. But the house I share with Harmony is full of things like shrunken heads and ceremonial hoods, so I don't throw a lot of judgment around.

Harmony did everything she could to let me know that optimism is a synonym for stupid the second I walked in the door back home. It didn't matter that I told her I was a grown-ass woman, and I could make decisions about who I married–and when. Harmony had never liked Bobby, and when she found out I married him on the quick, she was so mad I thought she was going to try and ground me, like I was sixteen again and sneaking out with Tony Smercizivic. But I wasn't. I was forty, and Bobby was "the one."

He was.

Okay, here's where my optimism admittedly verges into the realm of...not quite stupidity, but definitely a touch of naivete, along with more goodwill for humanity (particularly men) than they might actually deserve. It's because I'm

Cancer on the fifth house Cusp, we are highly emotionally loyal to those we love.

Which is why it was such a punch in the gut to discover that Bobby was living as a loving and devoted husband to three women. Only Bobby could have that much nerve. Only Bobby could so completely and absolutely blind-side me. Which makes me sad. For him...and for me. And his other two wives. We all put our faith in him.

Being mad about the fact that my one and only husband was a polygamist and kind of a dirt bag still isn't factoring into my emotional range now that he's dead. I'm just sad, the kind of overwhelming sadness that hollows out your belly and makes you believe that you'll never be hungry again, never want anything again, never feel anything again.

The other two wives join me and we all stare down at the pieces of the *talentum*.

"Nico says to each take our own piece and guard it with our lives," Helena says.

Nico is the private eye she hired just today to find out if Bobby was cheating on her. She didn't end up needing him to solve that mystery, but having him on speed dial did turn out to be helpful. He was the one who told us about the Hydra and that it would disappear Bobby's body for us.

"That may not be easy. I already had someone try and take mine," Maddie admits in a quiet voice. "Right before I came here."

Bending, I pick up my piece and hold it close to my chest. "We'll keep it secret, even from each other," I start to say when Helena interrupts with a snort.

"Even from each other? We're never talking again after this."

I'm pretty sure that's not true, but Helena's the type who can't be told she's wrong. She'll just have to figure it out on her own. "Hide the piece the best you can," I say. "This thing is clearly powerful and dangerous. We wouldn't want it to fall into the wrong hands."

"Yeah, like Bobby's hands," Helena snarks.

"There's people out there worse than him," Maddie says, but then adds in a tired voice, "Probably."

I put my piece of the *talentum* into the trunk of my Soul and watch as the two other wives retrieve theirs as well. After that, the three of us end up going out for drinks, Maddie mourning her husband, me memorializing mine, and Helena flat out celebrating his death. She insists that it's time to get mind-altering drunk.

I've had my mind altered many times. Harmony is a proponent of opening your mind to the doors of perception through various psychotropic substances. But drinking with your sister wives after watching your husband die is a whole new astral plane, even for me. Still, it is kinda fun. I hope we can hang out again sometime, maybe when we haven't just finished disposing of a body.

More than a little drunk, I head home feeling lost, unanchored, a true widow.

Harmony strips me down, dunks me in a hot bath of chamomile and lavender, then dresses me in a pure white cotton shift and tells me to go to bed for a week.

She doesn't say, "I told you so." She isn't petty like that. She doesn't have to be. Without saying anything aloud the words hang in the air between us. Luckily, they're accompanied by a fierce love. Whatever happens, I know that Harmony will always be there for me.

Despite Harmony's bath and homemade sleep tea, I lie in bed for a long time unable to fall asleep as the events of the night replay themselves over and over again. I have a strong feeling that this isn't the end, but only the beginning of something. Something big.

And right here and now, I make a vow to myself that the next time I get called into battle, I'm going to come out of it victorious.

1

NEARLY ONE YEAR LATER

One of the truest things I know about myself is that I love weddings. Big elaborate ones in ballrooms, small intimate ones in sunlit fields, and even the totally bonkers one that took place in the center of a mosh pit during a Rage Against the Machine concert. Whether the bride and groom were shouting their vows or reciting them from a Klingon translation—I always feel moved.

Tonight, at Maddie's wedding to Aden, it should be no different...but it is.

I want to do the Chicken Dance, Electric Slide, and the Macarena with a full heart and light feet, the way I usually do at wedding receptions, but instead I find myself losing focus halfway through "Y.M.C.A."

Usually I add energy to the dance floor, my enthusiasm spreading to everyone else.

Usually my dancing is effortless and spontaneous.

Usually I dance until my feet hurt and then I dance some more.

But tonight, I'm not quite feeling it...and it's not just because the wedding was interrupted by a mega-billionaire bent on world domination who tried to kill all of my friends. Don't get me wrong, that was definitely a blot on the day, but like all dark clouds, it eventually passed and the sun shone through once more.

Why then is a part of me still cold at heart?

Well...it's probably because that mega-billionaire is almost certainly coming after me next. No matter how many deep healing breaths I take, I can't quite shake the sense of impending doom.

But I have to. At least for a few hours. I mean, you just can't spend all your time worrying about annihilation from a crazed bazillionaire. Also, this is Maddie's big day and being a guest at her—or anyone's—wedding is a privilege. Witnessing the love two people share is a reminder of the best part of the human experience—finding and connecting with one's soulmate.

Okay, sure, my own soulmate search didn't end well. But I am not going to let Bobby's betrayal make me bitter. I saw Helena go through that, and it was rough. I'm also not going to doubt myself or my ability to know how to love like Maddie did.

Instead, I am just going to keep breathing and remind myself that the winds of lady fate will steer me in the right direction.

I just wish she'd hurry up with it. It's tough being stuck on the sidelines while my sister-wives (this is what I call them, although they both hate it) gain powers and find their true loves. Not that it's been easy for Helena and Maddie. Their magical powers developed on their birthdays, powers that aligned with their horoscope.

Maddie, a Gemini, could split herself into twins, and each twin could split as well, meaning that she could be in more than one place at a time. She claimed it was super useful with her four kids, but it turned out to be even more convenient when Geoff Busk, a tech guru and quadrillionaire came after us all. He knew about the *talentum* and its ability to bestow godlike powers, and he wanted it.

I don't know any other uber rich people, so I can't say they're all like this, but Busk reminds me of a spoiled toddler—if he wants something, he expects to get it. In this case it meant threatening the lives of Maddie and her children. Maddie got really pissed off and killed a bunch of goons—with some help from her demigod boyfriend (now her husband!). Yet despite giving it their all, Busk got the *talentum* piece.

He came after Helena next, by framing her for murder. That messed Helena up pretty bad. She seems cold and like the type who'd find her one-night-stand dead beside her in bed and just shrug it off with a mental reminder to have her housekeeper change the sheets. In reality, it shook her to the core. It didn't help that the scandal of it all led to her losing her hotshot lawyering job.

That Busk is a weasel and a spoiled baby, but he's not a total dummy. With Maddie, he'd used her kids against her, threatening their lives. With Helena, it was her career.

Still, things had worked out okay for Helena in the end. She has the power to create earthquakes big enough to break the Richter scale, and equally importantly—she finally found love. Helena might have lost her part of the *talentum*, but she gained the actual Casanova (a hottie professor who goes by the name Ford these days), who's vowed to settle down and be true to her and her alone.

Now, though, with Maddie and Helena's pieces of the *talentum* gone, it's pretty obvious that Busk is going to come after me next. It'd be nice if he'd wait until I get my powers on my birthday—it's only three weeks away. Actually, a few days after my birthday would be even better. I don't even know what those powers will be and judging from what Maddie and Helena went through, I'm guessing it'll take me some time to figure out how best to use them.

"Y.M.C.A." finally ends and I push my way to the edge of the dance floor as a slow song begins. As a single lady at a wedding, pop culture tells me I have two choices for how to behave. I can sulk on the sidelines, angry at the world because love has done me wrong. Or I can be a horny single looking for a hottie to take home for the night.

Luckily, Harmony always taught me that as women we have more choices than the world (mostly the men half of the world) tells us. So I've always seen slow dances as a chance to make new friends. I take pleasure in finding the people at the edge of the crowd, the grandpa with a cane or the shy and awkward teenage boy, and I coax them into joining me on the dance floor.

Now my gaze goes to the tall dark figure standing just outside the circle of lights.

Roar, the Viking berserker who had been guarding Helena's piece of the *talentum*. I went on a little road trip with Helena and Ford to hunt him down, where he lives in the wilds of New Hampshire, totally off the grid. And we found him all right. Naked as an animal of the forest, in all his bare glory.

And it was glorious. I've always considered the human body a work of art, but Roar's is something on a whole different level. He's large and muscled and...hung like a horse.

Of course he's fully dressed right now, but even in a borrowed suit he looks amazing.

As if he senses me staring, Roar takes a step forward, just enough to light his eyes so that I can see he's watching me too.

Given that he lives off-grid and has only displayed the barest communication capabilities, I'm not sure if he realizes that we're in a rom-com right now, each of us gauging the other to see if we should ask for the dance.

Too bad he's already bluntly told me he only looks at women as places to drop off his berserker seed. I'm pretty sure our vibes are probably not on the same wavelength. I'm thinking about cute, flirty dialogue, and maybe some punch afterwards while we share childhood stories; he's thinking impregnate, impregnate, impregnate.

Despite myself, my heart picks up speed.

Everything in me urges me to cross the floor, take his hands, and lead him to the dance floor. Normally I listen to my inner voice. It almost never steers me wrong—although I was wrong about Bobby, I believe that he was meant to be a part of my life's journey.

Roar, though...I'm a little bit afraid of him. I've seen him go into his berserker rage; his eyes roll back and become milky white. Then it's like his soul escapes, leaving behind all humanity and in its place only a killing machine remains.

A part of me wishes I could be how Helena used to be and separate sex from love. Have one-night stands and no-strings-attached sex. Then I could have just one night with Roar and his beautiful body.

But I'm not that person. I need a soul connection before I can even think about sex. Okay...well maybe I can think about it. I mean, I am thinking about it with Roar, but that's as far as it will go.

He matter-of-factly informed me of his animal husbandry mentality when it came to women when we first met, which shouldn't have been surprising because he's a bit of a Nean-derthal. The surprising thing is that I'm attracted to him despite that—normally that type of thinking is a total turn off for me.

I guess sometimes the pheromones are stronger than the brain when it comes to desire. But I still get to decide whether to act on that desire.

And I'm not going to.

Not tonight.

Not ever.

Instead of relief, the decision comes with a little sigh of disappointment.

Nevertheless, I break eye contact with Roar, looking down at my hands and more specifically at the wedding ring still on my finger. Maddie and Helena ditched their rings almost right away, but I've kept mine on. They'd worn theirs for so long that even without the ring there was a spot on their fingers where it had worn a groove into the skin. My ring had barely twenty-four hours on my finger before Bobby was dead.

Now, Maddie is sporting a new ring from Aden to cover up the dent that Bobby had left in her life—and on her finger. Helena and Ford aren't tying the knot yet, but the groove in her finger had never been as deep as Maddie's. She said she always took it off to work out and lift weights, but I think there's more to it than that. I don't know if Helena ever truly let Bobby in, not the way Maddie did, warm, and welcome, with arms widespread. I can see that Ford is already more integral to Helena's life than our shared husband ever was... and maybe that's true for Maddie, too. The way she looks at Aden tells me that he's not just a replacement for Bobby; he's the guy she was meant for all along.

And while I'm the mystical one of the group, somehow, fate hasn't steered me in the right direction yet, even though I'm always open, always listening, always willing. I thought that's what Bobby was—the beginning of everything, a long story that wouldn't end until we were on a spiritual plane together, united in so much more than just our earthly bodies.

I think that's why it's so hard to let go. Bobby and I were at the very beginning of something, but then we skipped the middle and went right to the end. It left me discombobulated and I needed time to process it. But now I think I'm ready...ready for the first, small step.

Giving the ring a twist, I slide it off my finger and then into my pocket. When I get home, I'll put it in a jar with some arrowroot powder for purification and healing. Maybe eventually I'll wear it again and it will be a reminder of the good times Bobby and I had...although not on the same finger.

For most people taking a ring on or off is a small thing, but for me. it's huge and I can actually physically feel my heart lighten. And as it does, my gaze once more turns in Roar's direction...but this time he's not looking back at me.

Instead he's in a tight clinch with Maddie's sister, Stef.

Stef is one of those people who constantly needs attention —preferably of the male variety. Maddie told us that she used to flirt with Bobby all the time and that she wouldn't be surprised if it went beyond that behind her back. Helena offered to find out, but Maddie said she prefers not to know. I'm all for women owning their sexuality, but for some reason, Stef doesn't scream that she respects herself. She uses her body as a tool to get attention, and throws herself at any man who gives it to her.

Stef has been on the prowl all night. It's been sad watching her trying to get Aden's attention, when it's clear he doesn't have eyes for anyone other than Maddie. She also threw Ford a wink and Helena wasted no time shutting that down. She told Stef that if something was in her eye, she'd be happy to take it out for her.

Now, she's clearly found the one hottie who isn't attached to anyone and she's set her sights on reeling him in.

And he doesn't seem to be putting up a fight, even as I watch his arms wrap around her and he takes a step back further into the shadows.

I stand abruptly, my chair tumbling to the ground behind me, ready to march over there, pull her off him, and—

Do nothing. Because Roar is not mine. And I don't want him. Or I do...but not in a way that I can live with.

Deliberately, I turn away and instead head for the place where I last saw my shoes. It's time to put them on and head home.

2

————————

"Harmony!" I shout as I get home from Maddie's wedding. I have to tell my mother everything that happened, starting with Helena's powers manifesting—because that's the good news. Knowing my mother, though, she'll be more focused on the bad news—that Busk now has two pieces of the *talentum*.

If he gets the third and is able to perform the ritual...it's anyone's guess what he'll do with the power of a god, but I'm guessing the betterment of humankind isn't at the top of his list.

Harmony already declared that Busk had the worst aura of anyone she'd ever seen and the damage he would do to the world would be astronomical. She also said he would get my piece over her dead body and when she says things like that, she means it. Literally.

When I tried to remind her that this was my problem and my fight, she just scoffed. It's a sound I know well because

I've been hearing it my whole life. That scoff means that I'm in way over my head and that I need to step back—preferably behind her—so that she can protect me.

When I was a kid this was comforting. As a teenager, a little embarrassing—especially the time Harmony took it upon herself to tell off the girl who had been bullying me. At some point in my adult years, I probably should've made her stop.

But the thing is that when Harmony is fired up about something, it's hard to get through to her. She's too busy mixing potions, muttering hexes under her breath, and telling me to get out of the way. If there's something wrong, Harmony is going to fix it—and that means going temporarily blind and deaf to the world while she does.

She's never been able to hear me say, "Hey, I got this."

Sure I could've pressed the point before I hit forty, but it would've led to a fight and I hate fighting with Harmony. It fills the house with bad energy that doesn't dissipate for days no matter how much sage I burn.

This time, though, I'm going to make Harmony listen. I'm a grown woman and even though she thinks that I'm totally hopeless and helpless, I know that's not the case.

Or I guess I hope it's not the case.

And if it turns out that I'm hopeless and helpless after all, I'm not going to run and hide while my mother goes up against an evil moneybags bazillionaire. Once she hears about his attack today, it's going to take everything in me to keep her from shoving me out the door and off to Faerieland right away. She already has my go-bag packed, along with directions to a portal to Faerieland where she thinks I'll be safe from Busk.

"Harmony!?" I yell again, moving through the house.

Harmony hasn't responded and for a moment I consider sneaking up to my room and letting our showdown wait until tomorrow when I have more energy. But no, trouble is coming and she'll just see me as even more helpless if I don't tell her about it right away.

"Harmony!" I take off my heels and rub my feet. I prefer a good boot or sandal to a heel, but I wasn't going to wear Birkenstocks to Maddie's wedding.

I wander the house in my blue dress. "Harmony!?" She must have gone out. I change into a flowy summer dress. It's nice to feel free after that tight blue one.

The doorbell rings and I turn, wondering who it could be. But I think a part of me already knows, because I'm not surprised when I open the door to find Roar standing there.

"Why are you here?" I ask the Viking. I have to bite my tongue to keep from asking if he already finished ravishing Stef. Did he toss her away like a used tissue, or is she waiting for him in the car? Except there is no car behind him. I realize; there is, however, a large, gray horse.

I blink at it, wondering if there's a gas leak in the house causing me to hallucinate. But no, the stallion remains.

"Where did the horse come from?" I ask.

"I rode it here," Roar answers simply. Then holding out my phone he adds, "I was sent, with this..." As I reach forward to take it, he pushes past me into my house. "The one-eyed werewolf told me to bring it to you."

Nico, the private investigator Helena has on retainer, had taken all our phones and distributed them among friends and family members, then sent them all on road trips, hoping to throw Busk off our scent as we went to retrieve Helena's piece of the *talentum* from Roar.

"Come right in, why don't you?" I huff as Roar shoulders past me. I bet Helena and Maddie orchestrated this. They think that I need help in the love department. But Roar... there's no denying the attraction; just the slightest brush against him sends his scent up my nose and then zinging straight down to yoni.

Again I can't help but wonder at the effect he has on me. I've never before been into the ultra-masculine muscled type but it's clear that his body is communicating with mine in a way that's easy to interpret—SEX SEX SEX SEX SEX. It might as well be a flashing neon sign.

I rub my nose, trying to clear the pheromones that are clouding my brain and focus on understanding why—and how—Roar is here.

"Did you steal someone's horse?" I ask.

Roar had been looking around the house, but now he swings toward me, obviously offended. "A Viking would never take another man's horse."

"What about a woman's?" I can't help myself from asking, in a much snarkier tone than usual. It's not like he's the first unenlightened man I've ever come across. He's just the first I've felt the need to try and educate. If only good pecs indicated a similarly stacked level of enlightenment.

Roar looks confused by this. "A woman's horse would be too small for me. I am a large man. And women are—" He gestures to me, as if all women are my size. I mean, I am average-sized, but that doesn't mean I stand for all women. Although maybe in Roar's eyes I do. Maybe all women are just interchangeable to him.

I find the thought more distressing than I like. Helena kept insisting Roar was making eyes at me when we met at his cabin a few days ago...but maybe that's just how he looks at anything feminine. The only reason he didn't give Helena the hairy eyeball was because she belonged to his friend, Ford.

If there's anything Roar honors, it's man code. He probably looks at Helena as Ford's actual possession, not that they've entered into a mutually beneficial relationship.

"The horse is mine," Roar says, interrupting my thoughts. "Velvet Thunder is the best stallion I've ever ridden."

"Oh," I say. "But how did—" The name gives me pause, and nearly a bad case of the giggles, but I overcome it. "Velvet Thunder get here—not here to my house," I quickly clarify, "But to you, at the wedding?"

"At a fast trot, I assume."

I narrow my eyes at Roar, certain he's being deliberately dense. "He ran from New Hampshire to New Jersey?"

Roar shrugs in response. "It's not so great a distance, if one is loyal."

"I've just never before heard of a horse that came looking for its owner so...steadfastly," I say, talking more to myself than to Roar.

"Really?" Roar frowns, considering this. "I never had a horse that didn't." Matter-of-factly he adds, "We have a soul connection."

It takes everything in me not to give a coo of awe at this. I can resist a man who's nice to look at, but one who can charm horses and talks about his bond to them...that's the type of stuff that I find irresistible.

Which is no good, I remind myself yet again. He might love his horse, but he still hasn't shown any sign of understanding that women have souls, too—or that he's interested in us for anything other than our ponytails and hindquarters.

"Are you riding him back to your cabin?" I ask him, with the subtext being 'when are you leaving?' I drove him to New Jersey but I don't want to volunteer to take him all the way home to New Hampshire. Being trapped in a car with him for that many hours would not be a good idea. Especially if it's followed up by being alone with him in the woods, where he mostly seems to run around naked.

I shiver.

His eyes are on me and I try to pretend I wasn't just thinking about his nude body. He tilts his head. "I cannot leave yet. I failed in my duty. I must set it right."

"Your duty?" I ask. "You mean to the *talentum*?"

Roar nods. "I should not have given it back to Helena. She is fierce and brave, but still—a woman."

Gritting my teeth with irritation, I turn on my heel and head into the kitchen, needing to put some space between myself and the sexy, infuriating, Viking that is Roar.

3

———————

Roar, of course, follows me.

The chain of custody for Helena's piece of the *talentum* is a bit confusing. She handed it off to Nico to keep it safe. In turn, he gave it to Ford, knowing he has a whole special storage area for magical antiquities. Ford, though, realizing things were getting hot and that Busk would go to great lengths to get it, decided it needed even more protection than even he could give. That's when he passed it along to Roar.

By the time Helena showed up to claim it from Roar she was three people removed from it and he saw her as an attacker, not realizing she was the original owner. Once he calmed down and was no longer in his berserker rage, he and Helena had a ceremony (which involved chugging mead) to officially take responsibility away from Roar and put it back into Helena's hands.

I can't resist calling over my shoulder, "The *talentum* decided Helena was worthy, and I think that means more than what the hired security specialist thinks."

"But she still lost it," Roar insists stubbornly.

"Technically Ford lost it," I correct. "He left it in the car. And maybe it was for the best," I can't help but add. "Busk wasn't going to stop until he got his hands on it and the only reason his people retreated so quickly was because they found it."

Roar grunts. "We could've taken them. The fight had barely begun."

Spinning back around I find that Roar is directly behind me, and I bounce right off his chest. I stumble and would've landed on my butt if Roar didn't grab hold of me.

"Clumsy," he says patronizingly, setting me back on my feet.

"Rude," I shoot back, jerking away from his touch. And then, poking a finger into his chest, I add, "And for you that fight might've just been starting, but there were a lot of innocent people around who could've been hurt or killed if it had gone on."

This actually seems to get through to him. His brow furrows. Finally he says, "The innocents could have been protected. Ford failed the *talentum*, but I will not."

"He didn't fail it!" I exclaim, not even sure why I'm still arguing with Roar. Maybe because it's the most alive I've felt in a long time. "We don't know what's going to come next. This might all be part of fate's plan! He did after all put a magical tracking spell on Helena's piece, so at least we have that."

Roar crosses his arms over his chest, a gesture I already know is a sign that he is not convinced. "Vikings don't let fate decide future. We use might to make it as we will it."

I roll my eyes at this, wishing Harmony would wake up so she could hear this nonsense. But I don't need her here to know what she'd say, "You can be fate's tool or fate's fool," I tell Roar. And then add, "And Ford knocked you out with a single punch, so I don't think you should be acting like you're so much better than him."

"He knocked me down, not out," Roar counters. "And only because I was not fully beneath the berserker rage."

"You weren't?" I ask, genuinely curious. From what I could tell he looked pretty lost to the world, with his eyes rolling back into his head and going scary white.

"No," he answers shortly. "You would all be dead if I had not been fighting back the demon." There's a bitterness to his voice that I hadn't heard before now. And Roar's fists are clenched, but I can tell he's not angry at me. Everything in him seems to be focused inward, as if he's dealing with some enormous hurt that exists deep inside.

Even though I want to know more about the demon, I don't have it in me to ask questions when I can see he's so sensitive about it. Instead I pull out one of the kitchen chairs and point him toward it, then put the kettle on. "Some tea might help. And if not, I've got a bottle of gin in the cabinet."

"This is an impressive bloodstone," Roar comments. It's the first thing he's said since his arrival that is just nice easy small talk kind of stuff, and I'm relieved to have a break from all the stress of going back and forth with him. I don't think

I ever once said a cross word to Bobby and I've exchanged almost nothing but that with Roar.

Now I glance at the centerpiece Roar complimented, a two-pound bloodstone meant to boost emotional endurance.

Harmony had ordered it when I was in high school and dating Tony Smercizivic, who'd already knocked up three underclasswomen. In order for bloodstone to work along with the natural cycles of your body, you're supposed to wear it as jewelry. But Harmony claimed she needed the entire two pounder to counteract her emotions whenever Tony walked in the house, and instead she kneaded it like bread dough the entire time he visited. I swear she changed the shape of that stone in two months, which was all the time Tony had to give me.

But she didn't need to worry. He dumped me shortly after I gave him a monologue about how a woman's menstrual cycle is actually considered a powerful ingredient in blood magic by many Native American tribes, some Asian cultures, and also the Egyptians. Apparently Tony was more good old-fashioned Jersey than anything, because he was out of the car quicker than I could get my panties back on.

Over twenty years later, Harmony hauled the massive blood-stone back out the first time I brought Bobby home, no doubt hoping that I would spot it. I couldn't miss it, since she put it at the center of the table, replacing the moon cycles shadow lamp. I'd come back to the table after seeing Bobby to the front door to find her arranging a lace doily underneath the bloodstone, casting me a dark glance and muttering a string of words that I'm pretty sure was a Mayan prayer against evil.

Again I wonder where Harmony is and what she'll have to say about Roar.

"Just going to check my messages," I tell him.

As the kettle boils, I almost drop my phone when I see a video from Harmony. She rarely uses her cell and then only to make voice calls. She barely texts; I didn't even think she knew how to use the camera app.

"Is something wrong?" Roar asks.

"I don't know yet," I admit. He stares at me as I push play. Harmony's frantic voice echoes through the kitchen. On the video, the camera angle is low and wobbly.

"Crystal, they're here. They overpowered my wards. They know I have the *talentum*—" The video cuts away as the phone falls to the floor, but my mom is still yelling. "He can't do anything until the night of your birthday. That's when the *talentum* will reset and—" Someone picks up the phone and turns it off.

I play it again and again. "This woman...?" Roar asks.

"My mother," I say as I sink to the floor. Roar kneels beside me.

"We will get her back. Does Busk want to trade for your piece of the *talentum*?" Roar smiles but there is no joy in it—only the promise of pain and destruction. "We can use it to lure him to us and then I will crush the life from his puny body."

I shake my head. "You don't understand. Harmony has my piece of the *talentum*."

"Then we will get both back," Roar says. He lifts me to my feet. "I swear on my honor I will help you. I vow to protect you."

I look up at him, into his blue berserker eyes that I've witnessed go milky white with battle rage. It was scary seeing that happen. I wonder if it's scary for him, losing control like that? Or maybe he likes it? I know that I don't, no matter how hot it is to have him vow to protect and help me. And save my only remaining family member. Okay, maybe it's a lot hot.

Still, I've never understood the point of getting angry like that. Sure, I've lost my temper. Once as a kid I was so mad at my best friend that I told her that karmic justice would get her. Of course, I calmed down and took it back five minutes later. That's about the longest that I can hold a grudge.

Or it was. Because right now the idea of Busk hurting Harmony fills me with a hot flood of rage like nothing I've ever felt before.

"That's a nice offer, Roar," I say, absently giving his chest a little pat. "But it's Busk who's going to need protection. From me."

Luckily, Roar doesn't laugh in my face at this. If Harmony was here, she'd have definitely scoffed. I can almost hear the exact way she does it, like she's clearing her throat and heaving a giant sigh at the same time. It's always annoyed me, especially since the scoff is usually being directed at me, but now I would give anything to have Harmony back.

The anger that had been keeping my spine straight disappears as quickly as it came, leaving only grief in its place. Busk is a bad guy and he's made it very clear that he doesn't play nice. And yet, despite that, Helena gave him quite the spanking today. He had to be carried away by his goons and there was no missing the fact that he'd pooped his pants in fear. It doesn't take a top psychologist to guess that his ego will be smarting from that, or that he'll want revenge.

If he takes his wrath out on Harmony—

The anger flares again—even higher—before flickering out as the tears start to flow.

"Uh-oh," Roar says.

I flap a hand at him, shooing him away. "Go make the tea. I need to cry this out."

Holding in your emotions is just as bad as holding in your pee. Except a UTI can be cured with a round of antibiotics, but emotional backup can cause a lifetime of damage. I've always been emotionally regular because I don't hide anything. When I feel something, I let myself feel it.

Right now I'm feeling terrified for Harmony...although that thread of anger is still coursing beneath it. But the fear has the upper hand and I let it out in a round of heavy sobbing.

I sit, crying and staring at the bloodstone sitting in the middle of Harmony's table. She must have known I was going to need it to focus my feelings.

My optimism has gone out the window, and even I have to admit that if I tried to find a cheery thought right now, it would come off as decidedly manic. My piece of the *talentum* was the last that they needed.

Harmony had said she would take care of it, shroud it in spells and do everything she could to stop it from sending out magical signals that would draw Busk and his goons. She shrunk it down so that she could wear it on her finger. It just looked like a clunky hippy ring, the kind Harmony has dozens of. And I let her. I let her take on the burden of the *talentum*. This was the one time I should've put my foot down and insisted on taking care of myself.

But Harmony was so certain, and as much as I hated to admit it, Harmony has never been wrong before. From Tony to Bobby, her instincts were always dead on.

Except this time, she'd overestimated herself. We didn't know then who we were up against.

Harmony is gone and I'm left staring at a massive bloodstone and trying to think what I should do next. The last of my optimism drips away. Geoff Busk has the first two pieces of the *talentum*. Now he wants the third—and he's going to use Harmony to get it.

And knowing my mother, she'll let him break her before she'll hand it over.

4

I'm wiping away my tears by the time Roar slides three different cups of tea in front of me. Black Irish, green, and an herbal blend. Before I can say thank you, he disappears and a moment later returns with the sugar bowl and milk.

"I wasn't sure what you liked," he says hesitantly.

"I like all of them," I assure him. "Thank you."

He nods, looking relieved, but I don't know if that's because I'm happy with the tea or if he doesn't have to deal with my tears anymore.

"Now we will decide how to kill Busk," he says, taking the seat beside mine.

"Roar..." I put my hand on top of his. It's meant to be a comforting gesture, but the moment our hands meet I realize that was just an excuse to touch him. Every part of him—even his hairy toes—calls to me. If he was mine, I wouldn't have to find excuses to touch him...

But he's not, I quickly remind myself. And never will be. Just to send the point home, I ask Roar, "Did you sleep with Stef?"

"Stef?" He looks confused. Which doesn't mean he didn't get it on with her, it just means he can't be bothered to remember her name—or he never asked in the first place.

"Maddie's sister." Roar's brow remains wrinkled. "The blonde with the teased hair and micro-mini dress who wrapped herself around you at the reception. She made it very clear she wanted to get into your pants."

"Ooooh." Roar nods. "Stef. Yes, she wanted my seed very badly."

Jealousy, nasty and thick, curls in my gut. I hate the idea of Stef getting Roar's seed almost as much as I hate that smug look on his face as he talks about it.

"So?" I demand. "Did you give it to her?"

Roar stares at me hard, as if thinking something over. At last he says, "No."

Relief floods me, washing away that ugly lump of jealousy. Until Roar adds, "There was no time. You left and I had to follow. It's my duty to make up for my mistake and protect the last piece of the *talentum*."

"Oh," I say, feeling as if all the air has been knocked out of me. I'm getting emotional whiplash from all the changes. It was never like this with Bobby. With him I simply felt buoyant, like he and I existed inside a perfect dream. A short dream, I remind myself—and actually, kind of a total nightmare if I let myself think about the fact that the reason everything was perfect was because he was really, really good at lying. Still, never has another person gotten under my skin the way Roar does.

I wish Harmony was here. She'd tell him what's what. Then she'd tell me to take a nice warm chamomile bath and scrub until I've washed that man right out of my hair. If I could only just talk to her...

I stand abruptly, realizing that I *can* talk to her. Although it won't be easy.

"I need space! Roar, can you help move this?" I ask, gesturing to the heavy dining room table made of a solid slab of marble. Some people might buy something like that for fancy dinner parties, but Harmony mostly uses it for meditating—the marble helps focus her energies.

It took a crew of five guys and a dolly to get the table into its current spot but Roar walks over and using excellent form— lifting with his legs—he places both hands under the table and lifts it high into the air.

"Where do you want it?" he asks, not even sounding strained.

"Umm..." I look around wildly. Harmony and I share a more-is-more aesthetic and our little house is stuffed full of books, charms, and plants. Also furniture. That's where I turn my attention. Scooching around Roar, I put the coffee table on top of the couch and then push the two comfy reading chairs into a corner of the room. "Okay, right there, please," I direct, pointing to the space I just cleared.

As if he's carrying nothing heavier than a loaf of bread, Roar sets the table where I indicated. And I watch. In case he needs help, of course. And maybe also to see his muscles flex as he moves.

With that done, he turns to me. "What else can I move?"

Okay, I won't let myself think about how useful this man could be if I ever decide to not live with Harmony anymore. Or if I need to reach the coffee can, or am in desperate need of an orgasm.

"Nothing right now," I say quickly, banning any thoughts of orgasms.

I snag a piece of chalk from the kitchen counter and move to the space Roar just cleared. The wood floor here is old and scratched, all the varnish long since scraped away, which makes it perfect for chalk drawings. Tongue between my teeth, I get down on my knees and set to work.

I start with a spiral, the very first sacred shape I learned to draw as a young child. It's simple yet powerful. Now, though, I take my time with it, make the lines thick and the center of the spiral large enough to sit in. Once that's done, I draw a pentacle on the outer end of the spiral so that its energy will flow inside of it and to me.

"Magic," Roar says from behind me, his voice low with respect. I'm glad to hear it. If he was afraid or scornful, I'd have to send him away for worry he might bring the wrong elements into my spell. That would've been unfortunate because I need another person here to help me. And maybe also because the only part of seeing Roar leave that I'd enjoy would be the view of his perfectly formed backside.

"Yes, powerful magic," I confirm. "And that's not all of it."

With that, I head into the basement. It's a dark and murky space, but excellently organized by Harmony with everything labeled and sorted into plastic bins to protect from water damage when we get the occasional flooding. It takes me no time at all to find the amulet I need, along with a good strong rope. The amulet pulls magic out of any living creature that wears it and everything alive has some sort of magic in it. As Harmony says, "Just living is a type of magic."

Back upstairs, I stick the amulet into my bra—a move which immediately draws Roar's attention and a fiery blush. Then I tie one end of the rope around my waist and hand the end to Roar.

"Hold onto that," I tell him. As he's such a he-man type of guy, I expect him to start kicking up a fuss as I order him about, but I haven't seen even a flicker of resentment. Instead he does exactly as I ask without question.

Taking a breath for courage, I step into the center of the spiral, being careful not to smudge any of my chalk as I sit cross-legged at its center. "Okay, this is the tricky part," I tell Roar, as nervous butterflies begin to tickle my tummy. His gaze meets mine, focused and serious. It gives me the strength to continue. "I'm going to leave my body and meet Harmony on the astral plane to find out where she is and if she's okay."

Roar's eyebrows come together at this. "She will be ready to meet you?"

"No, she'll be ready to kill me." A nervous little laugh escapes me. "I've never done this before," I explain. "And it's not the safest thing to attempt. Harmony has magic powers so it's easier for her and she's honed her skills for decades.

She'll have no trouble hearing my call and meeting me. But I don't have any magic and well..." I shrug sheepishly. "She'd rather I not kill myself messing with powers that are beyond me."

This last is a direct quote, but I don't tell Roar that.

"You must do this?" he asks.

I think about the question for a moment, considering it. I suppose there are other options. I could tuck tail and run the way Harmony wants me to. I could go find Maddie and Helena—I know they'll do whatever they can to help—even if it means going after Busk himself. And with the magical tracking spell that Ford put on Helena's piece, that might even be possible.

But first I have to make sure that Harmony is okay. If she's not—I shake that thought off, refusing to give it a moment of my time.

"Yes," I tell Roar. "I must do this. Now."

"You will not die doing this," Roar says. It's not a statement, but an order.

"Not dying is definitely part of the plan." I smile at him, trying to be reassuring, but I can feel my lips wobble. "The amulet and sacred symbols will help me get there. While the rope—" I watch as Roar's knuckles go white as he tightens his hold on his end of it. "Will keep me connected to the physical world."

"I will bring you back," Roar promises, giving the rope a little tug as if demonstrating his strength. Of course, his strength isn't in doubt, but it'll also not be much help to bring my spirit back into my body if it gets lost.

I just have to make sure that doesn't happen.

Placing my hand over my chest where the amulet is tucked into my bra, I close my eyes and begin the chant that I've heard Harmony use. A floaty feeling, not unlike the one I get when I have a high fever, starts at the top of my head and then spreads to the rest of my body. It's not pleasant but it's not awful either. I continue chanting, not sure if I've made it through yet. Suddenly my ears pop, the way they do when experiencing a change in elevation.

I peek one eye open. Instead of seeing Roar framed by the kitchen doorway, there is...nothing. Just a sort of blue-ish tinged void. The rope around my waist trails off into the void and disappears.

"Hold fast," I whisper, knowing Roar won't hear me. I turn, floating in a gentle circle.

"Harmony?" I call. It occurs to me that I should've maybe tried to signal to her before leaving my body. It would stink to get to the astral plane and her not know I was there.

But she must hear my call. I think a part of Harmony must always be listening for my voice, which is comforting and kind of suffocating at the same time. She appears before me, her skin pale and tinged blue. I gasp. Her hands are tied behind her and a bruise blossoms across the left side of her face.

"Crystal! What the hell do you think you're playing at!?" she demands.

Ignoring this reaction, I walk, or well, float, towards her. "Are you okay? Did they hurt you?"

Harmony looks at the bonds around her wrists and shakes them off with an impatient gesture. They dissolve as they fall from her arms. Being experienced in the astral plane she can do stuff like that, which is pretty badass. She doesn't need an anchor either, like the one that I have with Roar. She can slip back into her body as easily as someone else slips on a shoe.

"I'm fine," she tells me. "I can take care of myself. But really, Crystal, do you have no sense? I told you the plan. Go to Faerieland and hide. I'll come find you when it's safe." She stalks toward me, clearly annoyed. "Instead you're playing around in the astral plane, so you can come and say hi to me."

"I'm not here to say hi," I huff like an angry teenager. "I had to make sure you were okay, and—"

"Well, I am. So go back home and pack your bags," Harmony interrupts.

I ignore her. "And," I continue, "to catch you up on what happened today."

"That Busk idiot already filled me in. He has two pieces of the *talentum* and is determined to get the third and perform the ritual. All the power will be his, there's no stopping him, and on and on and on." She rolls her eyes. "He sure likes to hear himself talk."

"He really does," I agree.

"Now that we're all caught up, it's time for you to vamoose. Remember, don't eat or drink anything in Faerieland. Don't make any promises. Don't—"

"Harmony!" I yell, totally annoyed now. "I've been to Faerieland before. I know the rules. Geeze."

She scoffs. "Never without me to keep you safe."

"I'm a forty-year-old woman; I can take care of myself," I say. And then add, "And I'm not going to Faerieland anyway. I'm coming to save you."

"No, you are absolutely—" She puts her head in her hands. "I need you to keep yourself safe. I'm not afraid of Busk, as long as I know you're not in danger."

"No matter where I go, I won't be safe," I tell her. "Not if Busk uses the *talentum* to become a god. You know it requires a human sacrifice, don't you? You should be afraid."

Harmony ignores this. "Look, Crystal, before you go. Busk is going to call you. Don't be stupid. Don't answer."

"I have to—" I start to tell her, but she interrupts.

"Then don't tell him we communicated. You are such a stubborn girl. If you won't listen to reason, then I have to tell you something else...about your birthday."

"My birthday?" My forty-first. It's in three weeks. One year from the weekend I took my vows with Bobby. One year from the night (technically the next day, early in the morning) he died.

Harmony looks nervous. She's never once been afraid to tell me anything. I can't remember a single time when she seemed anxious. She is always so confident. "You were born under a troublesome sky. So...I fudged the dates."

"What are you talking about?" I ask, confused.

"Your true birthday is sometime this week. I think before the day of the next blood moon. The day that Busk will want to perform the ceremony."

If I weren't already floating on the ethereal plane you could have blown me over with a feather. "You've lied to me my whole life about when I was born?" I ask. "And you don't know my actual birth date?"

Harmony read the stars. To do something like this was unthinkable. Is that why I never had the powers that Harmony did? Because I was working under the wrong planetary alignment?

"How could you?"

She actually looks ashamed. "I thought that I would never forget the day my beautiful daughter was born, but then after so many years lying about the date, the actual number slipped my mind."

"But why would you do this at all?" I demand.

"Your birth date had some very concerning planetary alignments, like nothing I've ever seen before. Knowing you were fated for something big, could've possibly changed your entire destiny. And..." Harmony hesitates.

"What?" I demand and then I realize that I don't need her to say it. "You wanted to protect me. Right? Just like you have all my life."

"Yes!" Harmony yells back. "Is that so awful? A mother wanting to protect her child?" Taking a deep breath, she adds, "Look, the good news is that Busk doesn't think that your powers will manifest in time to stop him. But they will. So you can use those powers to get away."

"I should leave you!" I shout, even though I never would. I know that my body here isn't solid, and I'm grateful that I can't cry. "You never believed in me," I say.

"I just wanted to protect you," she tells me. She floats toward me. Harmony suddenly stops, her eyes widening. "Your rope is fraying. You'll become unanchored from the real world!"

"What?" I say, but then look down at the rope still around my waist. It trails off into the endless smoky nether. When I got here it was solid, but Harmony is right, the rope is slowly spiraling apart—and with it my connection to the physical world.

5

———————

"Crystal!" Harmony scolds. "This is what I'm talking about! You never look before you leap! You have no sense. You need me to protect you—"

She reaches forward and smacks me on the forehead. It's like a full body punch from a heavyweight. And then I return to my body. Or I try to. Except instead of being inside it, I'm floating over myself while Roar performs CPR on my lifeless form.

"Come on," he urges. "Come back." I watch as he finishes compressions on my chest and then places his mouth over mine. He huffs a breath into my mouth and I taste mint. I've noticed that he keeps a little leather bag of herbs in his pocket that he sometimes chews on. I'd wondered what they were, if I'm being honest, had assumed the worst, that he was a tobacco chewer. Now I know. Mint.

I want more of it. And of him. Reaching up I wrap my hands into his hair and then sweep my tongue against his.

With a yelp, he jerks back, staring down at me in surprise.

"Hi," I say, waggling my fingers at him. "I'm back."

His light blue eyes darken with a new intensity. And then his mouth is on mine once more. This time, though, it's to give me a ferocious kiss, one that I meet with equal hunger. He wraps his arms around my body, lifting me off the hard floor and cradling me against his body—which is equally hard. It's amazing the different types of hard. While the floor made me stiff and uncomfortable, Roar's type of hard is perfect, as if he'd been carved out specifically to fit me.

With that dangerous thought, I jerk away, breaking the kiss. Roar, though, continues to keep my body flush to his. We both breathe raggedly as if we'd run a mile.

"Wow," I say. And then ask, "How do you know CPR?" It's not something I would've expected to be in his skill set.

"YouTube," Roar answers.

I look up at him in surprise. "You have internet at your back-woods cottage?"

"No, I go to the library," he answers simply. He has a way of making extraordinary statements sound as if they should be completely obvious.

"The library," I repeat like a dummy.

"Libraries have books..."

"You don't need to mansplain the library to me," I say.

"...and computers. It's a very useful place."

"I just..." I stop before I can admit that he didn't seem like a library type of person. Which would be a bit like saying I think he's not very smart. I've had enough people insinuate the same thing about me to know that doesn't feel very good. I feel ashamed for not knowing better. There are different types of smart than just the ones people usually recognize.

"Is that how you met Ford?" I ask, changing gears. "At the library?" Ford is a professor who specializes in magical antiquities. He's super-hot, but also a little bit nerdy. I definitely get the sense that he spends a lot of time in libraries.

"No," Roar answers. He shifts me into a cross-legged position, easily lifting me and then sitting me back down in his lap. I should object, at the manhandling and the assumption that I want to be cradled in his arms...except that I kind of like both of them. "I met Ford through the Immortal Men Support Group. We meet every decade or so."

Wow. To be a fly on the wall at one of those gatherings. If Ford and Roar are the example of their membership, it must be a lot of hotties in one room. I make a mental note to ask Helena if she knows anything about this group the next time I see her.

Before I can forget, I give Roar's chest a pat. "Thanks for saving my life," I tell him. "If you hadn't been here..."

"I was here," he says, cutting me off as if he can't bear to have me finish that thought. "I will always be here." My heart skips at this and I feel a flush rising, but then he adds, "Until the *talentum* is secure once more."

"Right," I say. "Of course." Taking that as my cue, I crawl out of his lap and stand on my own two feet again. "I'm not helpless, I don't need you to take care of me!" Or Harmony. "I am a strong woman. I am a warrior in waiting. I am—"

My phone rings and I let out a shriek of surprise.

Which is embarrassing. Roar raises his eyebrows at me. Clearly, I'm a little on edge right now. "Strong women can still scream," I say. "But fear doesn't define me."

Roar nods, as if that makes perfect sense.

I grab the phone, noting first that number shows as restricted. I answer and put it on speaker so Roar can hear.

"And then there was one," Busk says. The rat bastard. He's enjoying this moment, gloating.

"What do you want?" I spit.

"By now you realize that I've taken your mother," Busk says.

"You better not hurt her or I'm going to..." I stop. What can I do to him? Nothing.

"Your mother is fine," he dismisses me. And I can't exactly say I've seen the bruises. I agree with Harmony that they don't need to know that we communicated. "And as stupid as you play, you know what I want."

I blink, thinking. Harmony has the *talentum* on her. But if Busk still doesn't realize it, Harmony's warding spells are holding—the ring must not be emitting any sort of traceable magical signature. A shaky sigh of relief escapes me. At least this one small thing is in our favor.

"I may be stupid, but I know not to believe a word you say. Let me speak to Harmony," I order.

"I thought you might want to. She's right here."

Behind me Roar leans into the phone a growl of anger rumbling in his chest as if he wants to reach through the phone and pulverize Busk. Gently, I push him back. We need cool heads right now.

I hear a scuffle in the background, and then finally, Harmony's high pitched voice. "Crystal, if you give this micropenis man any—"

There's a sharp slap and Harmony's voice disappears.

"No!" I cry out at the same time that Roar reaches for the phone. I jerk it away before he crushes it.

"That's enough out of her," Busk sneers. "If she doesn't learn to watch her mouth, your mother will be coming home without any teeth. If she comes home at all."

A sob of horror escapes me before I can stop it.

"I will kill him for you. I swear it," Roar offers from behind me, which is sweet but not a lot of help right now.

Still, it helps me focus back on Busk. Harmony's playing the part, pretending she doesn't have the ring, but how long until they figure out the last piece of the *talentum* is on her?

"Tell me where the *talentum* is," Busk says, "and your mommy will be home right away."

"I...I don't know where it is," I say.

"You're lying," Busk says, calling me out immediately.

"Shit, look...I don't have it on me, and that's not a lie, but I can find it."

"I'm listening..." Busk says.

"I have this...it's like, radar. It's how we found Helena's piece...I sensed where it was."

"Crystal, what are you doing, girl?" Harmony yells. There's more of a scuffle and then some muted yells. I'm pretty sure they gagged Harmony.

"I'll trade myself for her." It's the best plan, really. Harmony has the *talentum*, so it's better that Busk has me than her. Plus, this is all my mess to fix. She shouldn't have to pay for my mistakes. "Take me and let her go," I say.

"No," Roar growls at my side.

I shush him. "Do we have a deal?" I ask

"Yes. Come to my Jersey Shore compound. I'll send some men to collect you."

"No," I tell him firmly. "I'll drive myself."

"I'll send you the address, then. Don't dawdle."

"And Harmony," I say, before he can hang up. "I'm not angry at what you did to me, what you told me the last time we talked. But I am angry you didn't tell me sooner."

"What's this?" Busk asks.

"Just wanted you to know, in case things go wrong. I love you."

"How sweet," Busk says. "But it sounds like you're trying to say something in code...so I'm gonna hang up now."

"I love you too," Harmony shouts. She must have ripped off her gag. "Crystal, if you have any sense, you'll run–"

The line goes dead and I stare at Roar.

"He's not going to let your mother go," he tells me.

"I know. But what can I do?" I ask.

I need help. I need Maddie and Helena.

6

Roar insists that we immediately get together with Maddie and Helena or, as he puts it, "call a war council."

I am equally insistent that we should wait until morning.

Maddie's wedding has already been ruined by an insane person, and Helena just become a goddess within the last twelve hours; they're likely both exhausted. Plus, it's Maddie's wedding night, and I'm not about to barge in on her and Aden with this new hell that Busk has stirred up for us.

"But he has already claimed her," Roar says, honest confusion on his face. "They have lain together, and will do so many times from now on. It is not a special night."

"It's still their wedding night," I stamp my foot. "And you've never had a wedding dress stripped off you, so you have no idea what you're talking about."

"You don't know that," Roar says, throwing me off for a second. But it's a quick second.

"Also..." I bring out the pointer finger and direct it toward Roar's nose. "it's called making love, not claiming your woman."

"Then Aden isn't doing it right," Roar sniffs.

While this certainly raises my interest, it also has my feminist red flags flying. Any hesitation I had about relegating Roar to the couch vanishes in that instant. We might have shared a little post-CPR snuggle, but that didn't change the fact that he only views me as his next possible berserker seed-starter, and any attachment he has to me is based solely on his vow to protect the *talentum*.

I shift the direction of my pointer finger from Roar to the couch in question. It's immediately obvious that there's a size differential between the two. Namely, the couch is tiny and Roar is not. The couch is mostly used for Harmony's clients while they wait for their sessions with her. She and I prefer floor cushions for when we're relaxing and watching television.

Nevertheless, I tell Roar, "This is where you'll be sleeping tonight."

He walks over to the couch and looks down at it, and then back up at me. "This is not big enough for us both."

Heat flares through me at his presumptuousness. "That's because we will not be sleeping together! I will be upstairs in my bed and you will be down here."

"No," he answers immediately. "I cannot protect you unless you are by my side. If danger comes I must be able to cover your body with my own."

My mouth goes dry at this image and the sensations I imagine would come with it. It takes a moment before I can muster a weak response. "You can sleep on the floor next to my bed and that is my final offer."

I turn off the lights and then start up the stairs with Roar at my heels. Despite myself it feels good to have him behind me; I hadn't quite realized how empty and quiet the house would feel without Harmony in it. Or how much Busk has shaken me. Being in the crosshairs of a power crazed megalomaniac millionaire has me shook.

Our house is a little Cape Cod and the upstairs bedrooms have sloped ceilings that I always felt gave my room the feel of a cozy hideaway. But with Roar squeezed in beside me, it's less cozy and more suffocating. Quickly, I point to the tiny spot of open floor beside my bed.

"You'll sleep there," I tell him.

"Good," he says, and immediately starts to shuck off his clothing. Because of course he sleeps in the nude. As tempted as I am to enjoy the show, I instead turn on my heel.

"I'll be right back with blankets and pillows," I say. From the hall closet I pull out a big fluffy feather stuffed pillow and a hand-made quilt a client gifted Harmony after she warned her to avoid a cruise that she found out ended with everyone on board coming down with an awful stomach bug. I know Roar will be comfy and warm with these and the thought makes me happy.

I freeze outside my bedroom door and consider putting the quilt back and exchanging it with the scratchy polyester one we use for picnics. But that would be mean. And it wouldn't really change anything—namely, that I care about Roar. Not just the way I'd care about any fellow human, but in a deeper way.

I care in a way that makes me want to find out his favorite fruit so when it's in season I can make sure to get it fresh-picked for him. I want to run my fingers through his hair with one hand while the other wields a pair of sharp scissors to snip off his split ends. I want to tuck the softest and best blankets around him and watch his face while he sleeps.

The way the women in my family show love is through care-taking...sometimes (Harmony, cough, cough) it can be suffocating, but at its best—it's little acts of love.

But I am not in love with Roar. I refuse to give in to my feelings. For once in my life I will not let my emotions rule me.

Shoving my shoulders back and lifting my chin up high—the way that Helena always does—I step into the room determined to not let Roar get to me. No matter what he says or does.

"I've got the bla—" I start to say, but cut myself off when I realize he's asleep. Every light in the room is on but he's snoring softly on the cold hardwood floor, lying on his side with only one of his gigantic biceps for a pillow. I remind myself that as a tough Viking warrior he's probably learned how to sleep anywhere and under any circumstances. Still... he doesn't look so tough right now, his face gentle with sleep. Despite myself my heart turns all gooey as I slip the pillow beneath his head and then tuck the quilt around his rock-hard body.

I know I shouldn't, but I can't resist taking one small liberty —pressing a gentle kiss to his forehead. He makes a mumbly sound that kinda sounds like "mmm," and then as I'm just about to sneak away his arm suddenly snakes out from beneath the blankets, unerringly finds my waist and pulls me in until I'm tucked tight against him. I struggle for a minute, but he just snuggles me harder, curling all his body around me so that I'm caged but not squeezed.

"Roar," I whisper, tapping at his arm. "Wake up. Let me go."

"Mmmph," he murmurs in response.

I'm pretty sure I could kick him in the cojones and he'd wake up pretty quickly. But even the idea of doing so makes me wince. His cojones are too pretty to even consider injuring them. And anyway, I realize as a gigantic yawn escapes me, being wrapped in Roar's arms is comforting. I'd been planning on taking a long chamomile bath to try and help me sleep, but I figured that no amount of herbs could let me have a peaceful night of rest—not while Busk has Harmony. In Roar's arms, though, it's possible to believe that everything will be okay in the end.

I have no idea how. But for the first time it seems possible.

Holding onto that thought, I fall asleep.

———

I wake the next morning with a gasp, sitting straight up in bed as everything returns to me in a rush of horror. "Harmony!" My heart thumps with terror.

I'd been having a dream that Busk had her suspended over a tank full of sharks and was slowly lowering closer and closer to it. I press a hand to my head, wondering if stress is maybe bringing out latent abilities to see the future. But then again...the sharks in the tank were all wearing suits and had Busk's face, and Michael Bublé was there too, singing "Somewhere Beneath the Sea," which seems to indicate that it was all just a weird dream and maybe I shouldn't read too much into it.

Still, it freaked me out.

And where the heck is Roar? I'm in my bed alone and he's...gone.

The place where he'd been sleeping is empty. The blanket is neatly folded and on top of my dresser along with the pillow.

He snuck out in the night...or early morning, without a word. Maybe he got a whiff of my morning breath and decided, *talentum* or not, he'd had enough of me. Or maybe Stef called him. That's ridiculous because Roar doesn't even have a phone, but even so, jealousy shoots through me. It's better, though, than the feeling of utter devastation that had been happening. I can't fall for Roar and I definitely cannot fall apart now that he's gone.

He's just a man. A hunky gorgeous man with a manhood worthy of sculpture...but a man just the same.

I don't want him and I don't need him.

Okay, I do want him. In the biblical sense at least. But that's not important right now.

I repeat "I don't need him" over and over as I shower, throw on clothes, and make myself a giant thermos of panda dung tea to go. The tea is Harmony's special blend, meant to open my mind. I figure if Harmony and I need to communicate mentally again, it might help me with the connection. My plan is to head straight for Maddie's house. It's only eight a.m., but I know she's an early riser.

As I back the Kia out of the driveway, I can't help but let a small sigh of sadness escape me. A part of me had been hoping that I'd get out of the shower and find Roar waiting in my room. Or that I'd come down and find him in the kitchen. But it's clear now that he's well and truly gone.

This early in the morning, our neighborhood is always quiet. There's just a lone jogger—old Mr. Furner with his legs so skinny his striped knee socks sag—and a big naked guy on horseback galloping straight at me.

I slam on the brakes at the same time that Roar's stallion skids to a stop in front of me, his front legs coming up the ground and then landing on the hood of my car.

"What the hell?" I demand, jumping out of the car.

"You were leaving?" Roar demands right back at me as he easily slides off Velvet Thunder.

"You left first!" I yell back.

Jogging in place, Mr. Furner stops beside me. "Crystal, this man bothering you?"

"No, Mr. Furner." I give him a smile. He's such a sweetie. "I've got this. You can go on."

Instead of moving along, he frowns. "Why don't I just go get your mother? Harmony will take care of him, no problem."

Gritting my teeth, I somehow manage to hold onto my smile. "I can take care of myself Mr. Furner. I'm a grown woman."

"Well, sure you are," he agrees and I think that's the end of it. But instead he gives me a patronizing pat on the arm. "But some women, like your mother, are made of steel, and some are softer." Just in case I'm not quite understanding, he spells it out for me. "You're the softer type, Crystal."

"Do not touch her," Roar says to Mr. Furner. "She is not yours to touch."

And that's when I lose it. "I'm not yours to touch either," I scream at Roar, with enough force to make him blink in surprise. Turning to Mr. Furner, I take it down zero notches. In fact I turn it all the way the hell up. "And you need to move along, Mr. Furner, or I am going to show you the type of steel I'm made of."

Without warning rain begins to fall. But no…it's not rain. A drop of it lands in my palm and I know it almost like it has a face and name just like Mr. Furner. This drop of water tells me that it was morning dew gracing the back of a blade of grass when suddenly it was lifted up into the sky and then released—falling into my hand.

"Holy shit, I did this," I say aloud.

For a minute Mr. Furner is so shocked he stops running in place and just stares at me, and then beyond me. Outside of the small circle that contains me, Roar, and Mr. Furner the ground is dry. Without another word, Mr. Furner backs away and then turns on his heel and jogs down the street without a single look back. If—no, when—Harmony gets back, I'm sure he'll be knocking at the door to tell her that he'd like us to keep all our magic nonsense within our own property lines.

But that's a problem for later. Right now I still have Roar standing in front of me. Unlike Mr. Furner, he's a little harder to scare away.

"I think maybe my powers are starting to manifest," I tell Roar. Focusing on the little bead of water still in my hand, I tell it to float. It doesn't move. I tell it to roll. Again, nada. I wipe my hands on my pants.

Maybe it was just a fluke.

"Here," Roar says, shoving a slightly damp white bag into my chest. "Bear claw."

I drop it on the ground in horror. "You went hunting?" Shaken, I look around. This is a residential area with a few wooded areas. I can't imagine it was easy to find a bear...

Roar's chuckle pulls me out of my head. "Hunting at the Whole Wheaterie Bakeshop," he says. "I saw you had some of their bread on your counter. They tell me bear claws are popular."

"Oh." Embarrassed, I bend to pick up the bag and then peak inside. A giant bear claw thick with white icing glistens back at me. I take a bite and it is delicious. Harmony isn't big on sweets in the morning—she says it doesn't give a body proper energy for the day. I hold the bear claw out to Roar. "Share?"

He shakes his head. "I bought a dozen. Velvet Thunder and I ate most of them."

"Oh," I say again. So Roar didn't go out to get me a treat, he and his horse needed food and I got the leftovers. I take another bite, although this one is a little less sweet. As I chew it occurs to me that Roar is wearing nothing but tighty-whities and tennis shoes, which must have raised some eyebrows. "You went into the bakery like that? Don't they have a no shirt, no shoes, no service policy?"

"Most businesses do," Roar admits. "But I find that most places—especially with women at the counter—will not mind the missing shirt." And with that he gives me a shit-eating grin.

Rolling my eyes, I take another bite of the bear claw, with perhaps a little more force than necessary. Why does this man make me so crazy? And even more importantly...why am I so ridiculously happy that he didn't leave me after all?

7

Riding a horse uses muscles you forget you have... or, rather, that you haven't used in awhile. I'm clenching my thighs tight, my arms wrapped around Roar's chest as he confidently maneuvers his stallion down Maddie's suburban street.

I wanted to take my Kia Soul, but Roar said he had already driven many hours inside my tiny vehicle and he would not do so again, or at least not until I tried his mode of transportation. My sense of fairness made me agree, despite suspecting it was a bad idea.

Like many little girls I went through a horsey-loving phase at one point in my life. But it's been years since I've ridden. And I never tried it bareback. Or while clinging to a half-naked berserker.

We gather more than a few curious looks, but I don't know if they are for the horse or for Roar, who refused to put on a shirt. He said that it would spook Velvet Thunder, which is ridiculous because the horse can't even see him while he's riding. Roar, though, insisted the two of them have a soul connection. After all the haggling over the shirt, I was surprised when he easily agreed to put on pants without much of an argument, at least at first. But then he showed up in nothing but chaps and I had to explain that those were not pants. After some heated wrangling, I told Roar to put on a pair of actual pants or I was driving.

Now my head bounces off his shoulder blades as he pulls Velvet Thunder to an abrupt stop outside of Maddie's house. It's early, but the front windows are open and the smell of bacon comes rolling across the freshly-cut grass. I know that Maddie relied upon her children to keep things in order around here during her marriage to Bobby. He was never around long enough to do much more than say hi to everyone and give her a few moments of marital bliss. Though apparently their sex life wasn't exactly blissful for her. But it looks like Aden has settled nicely into the role of suburban house-husband, even if he is a demi-god and the literal son of Hades.

Claiming his woman, my ass. Looks like Maddie claimed him.

I'd love to toss my head and slide off Velvet Thunder without a backward glance at Roar, but the truth is that I have no idea how to get off a horse. Roar had literally lifted me up and put me on the stallion's back when we left my house, which appears to be how the dismount is going to go, as well.

He jumps down and reaches up to me, easily lifting me from Velvet's back. I slide against Roar's smooth chest, my cheek brushing across his bare skin before my feet hit the ground, and there's a bounce in my step I can't entirely attribute to being a morning person as I walk to Maddie's front door.

I can't allow this to happen. Not only is this guy so clearly not my type, but I'm about to interrupt morning-after-wedding pancakes, and Harmony is in the hands of a megalomaniac. If I keep letting my clitoris do the thinking, we're all going to end up living in a world where Geoff Busk isn't just the richest person on the planet; he'll be a god, too.

And that is not a good thought.

"Maddie? Aden?" I call out, my hand resting on the door latch.

"Come in!" Maddie's voice sails through the house, and I walk in, happy to leave Roar behind for the moment, hitching Velvet Thunder to the mailbox. I need to be away from his musky self for a second.

"Hey!" I say, putting on a big smile as I walk into the kitchen. Aden is shirtless—why? Why is this a thing in my life suddenly? He has a smear of whipped cream at the corner of his mouth, along with a very obvious hickey on his neck. I spot one down closer to the waistband of his sweats as well, and I feel color rising in my cheeks.

"Is this a bad time?" I ask.

"What? No!" Maddie insists, sliding into her chair as Roar joins us. Maddie raises an inquisitive eyebrow at me, clearly hoping to find out that Roar and I spend the night in the same way that she and Aden did.

"Would you like some coffee?" she asks and to my ears it sounds like code for, *Did you two do the deed?*

"Yes," Roar says, at the same time I say, "no."

"He slept on the floor of my bedroom," I blurt out.

"In my arms," Roar adds with a satisfied smile.

"But not in a sexy way," I clarify.

"It was sexy," Roar objects. "Your bottom was tucked tight against my manhood."

"Roar!" I slap the table with annoyance. "That's true, we spooned. But our clothes were on." I remember that Roar was naked and quickly qualify, "My clothes were on. And," I add triumphantly, "Nothing happened except sleep."

Roar's smug look evaporates at this. He moves to the coffee pot, turning his back to me. "This is true. You needed rest more than you needed my seed."

Maddie and Aden share a glance, and I throw myself into a chair, ignoring their cutesy, silent communication. They look at me expectantly, but I don't know where to start. Asking how their night was seems a little superfluous, given the perfectly tousled look of Maddie's hair and...yes, those are scratches across Aden's shoulder blades. I'm about to abandon the situation altogether when Roar sets a cup of coffee in front of me, then downs half of his in one gulp.

"Your pleasure is over, and now it is time for war drums," he says.

"Okay, that might be a little brusque—" I object, but he cuts me off.

"We need the scary Valkyrie woman, as well."

"He means Helena," I say, serving as translator.

"What's going on?" Maddie asks, blowing away the steam rising from her coffee. She's still learning all of her wind powers, so it's a bit forceful and some coffee splashes into Roar's crotch. He jumps up, brushing off the liquid.

"Aren't you glad you wore pants now?" I ask him.

"Crystal's Harmony has been taken," Roar says, his irritation showing as he sits back down.

"Can't you restore that for her, buddy?" Aden asks, tipping me a wink.

"He means my mother," I say loudly, before anybody else can get a one liner in. "Geoff Busk has taken her as collateral. He wants my part of the *talentum* now that he has the other two. Only, he doesn't realize that he already has it. Harmony shrunk my ring down into a real ring, like a human-finger sized one, and she's wearing it."

I let that sink in. Busk already has all the pieces of the *talentum.*

"But can't he trace the magical signal?" Maddie asks. "That's how he found me and Helena when our powers manifested."

"Harmony has it covered for now," I say, waving away Maddie's concerns. Or at least this particular one. "She used her own magic to block the signal coming from the *talentum.* Busk has no idea that he already has it in his possession."

"Great!" Maddie says. "That's good news."

"Except we can't have it where he can get it. I've offered myself in exchange for Harmony."

There's a moment of silence, like they can't believe how stupid I actually am.

"Also...Harmony told me something. I thought that my birthday was in three weeks, but it's actually sooner."

Maddie eyes me over her cup. "How much sooner?"

"Funny story," I say with a little laugh that I have to force out. "Harmony can't actually remember."

"But..." I bite my lip. "I think my powers are maybe starting to manifest. I sort of made morning dew turn into a very small bit of rain."

"She almost ruined her bear claw," Roar adds, unhelpfully. I glare at him as he adds, "Although on the bright side she did scare away the fragile old man."

Maddie digests this information and then turns back to me. "Is it possible today is your birthday?" She gives a little smile. "Should I bake a cake?"

"I've got a better idea," Aden stretches, his muscular arms rippling. "I think the berserker is right. We need the scary woman."

8

———————

Helena shows up half an hour later with Ford in tow. They also are giving off waves of sexual exhaustion. Ford touches Helena's lower back and she accidentally erupts a dirtspout in the front yard that sends Velvet Thunder into a paroxysm.

"You must be more careful with your magic. My horse is not well pleased."

"Sorry," she apologizes to Roar from the front hallway, for the fourth time. "I've only been a goddess for less than twelve hours. I'm not good at this yet."

"You're good at other things, honey," Ford tells her, massaging her shoulders. "Excellent, in fact. And that was before gaining your powers."

"I'll remind you I'm also a lawyer," she says, playfully smacking his hands away. "You'll touch me when I allow it."

The six of us gather at Maddie's table while I get Helena up to speed on what's happened, and how Busk doesn't realize that he already has exactly what he wants—the last piece of the *talentum*.

"Then it's not just your mom's life at risk here," Helena tells me. "Sorry, but it sounds like she's actually quite ready to be the sacrificial lamb. Harmony knows this is bigger than her."

"What are you suggesting?" Maddie asks, her hand clasped in Aden's.

Helena shrugs. "Harmony knows the stakes. If Busk figures out that she has the *talentum*—and he will—then the whole world might as well hang it up. She wants Crystal to keep her distance."

"No," I say, my hand coming down hard on the table. "I don't care about the rest of the world; I want Harmony back. And the *talentum*. Busk has everything; why does he want more?"

"Because he's a dick," Helena says with a roll of her eyes that reminds me that even though she's found her goddess powers she can still be a bit of a dick sometimes too. "Who cares why he wants it? He's a sick person. We're not trying to fix him, we're trying to stop him."

"Why do I have to be the one to sacrifice something in order to stop him? Maddie got to save her family and get a new husband. Helena earned the most famous lover in the world, also, you kind of grew a heart in the process. But now Harmony is in danger and we're just going to be like, well... she's willing to throw herself in front of the train—why try to stop it?"

"That's not what we're saying, Crystal," Maddie says.

"It's what I'm hearing," I say, and my voice cracks as my mouth pulls down at both corners. Shit, shit, shit. I am usually all about letting my emotions have their way, but I do not want to cry right now, in front of the whole group. For some reason, I feel like I'm back in middle school, getting picked last for kickball and eating lunch alone in the corner.

It didn't feel good then, and it doesn't feel good now.

"I fought for you guys," I say, letting the tears overflow. "And now you've both got these awesome powers. It should be easier to win!"

"That's exactly where the problem is," Helena says, all matter of fact, even in the face of my tears. Maddie is wiping my face with a napkin, but Helena is staring me down, using logic to make me feel better.

"We've beaten him twice, that only means he's going to get cagier. And—what Maddie said about the *talentum* is still true. He has all kinds of tech ways to locate magical signals. Two demigoddesses coming at him in a frontal assault is only going to set off every klaxon he's got on his fortress of ass-itude. If we come at him point blank with all our powers, it will only drive him underground—and he'll drag Harmony with him."

I take the napkin from Maddie and wipe my nose. A twenty-four-seven mom, she'd probably do it for me if I let her. "So what are we going to do then?" I ask. "Because I am not letting him have Harmony. I don't care if that's what she wants or not. This one time, she's not getting her way —I am."

Helena gives me a hard stare. "This isn't woo woo touchy feely time, Crystal. That's what I'm trying to make sure you understand. If you go after Harmony you have to be ready to get blood on your hands."

My stomach heaves at this, and I press a trembling hand to it. "I understand that," I say in a small voice.

Helena doesn't take her eyes off me, until Maddie gives her an elbow in the side. "Easy," she says.

"No," Helena shakes her head. "We're not doing her any favors by not being honest. This is war now."

"She is right," Roar says and I try not to feel betrayed that he's siding with Helena.

"I haven't forgotten or forgiven what Busk did to me," Helena continues. "He killed someone to use as a pawn, he outed me as a supe, and tried to ruin my career. I made a vow to end him and I'm sticking by it."

Ford's hand lands on Helena's shoulder. "Wherever she goes, I follow. So I guess I'm in for taking Busk out too."

It's amazing watching Helena go from icy steel cold to gooey as she turns to look at Ford. "You don't have to."

"Yeah, I do," he answers. "You'd do the same for me."

Helena gives a little nod and this seems to settle it. My heart aches, wishing I could have that same connection.

"He threatened my children," Maddie says, her voice quieter than Helena's. "And if he becomes a god, I'm not sure what that will mean for their futures." Aden's hand covers Maddie's as she adds, "We're not letting that son of a gun get god powers. No way, no how."

"I have other people I can reach out to as well," Helena says. "We can bring this guy down."

Tears fill my eyes and my heart swells, knowing these people are in my life. "If you guys take care of Busk, then I can focus on rescuing Harmony." Then remembering the only part of a plan we have is me exchanging myself for Harmony, the teamwork high fades. "But how?"

"I have something that might help." Ford sets a tablet in the middle of the table. Not an iPad but an actual old world tablet made of stone. A jewel set into the stone blinks. Ford points a finger at it. "This shows where Busk is hiding with the *talentum*. And where he probably has Harmony hidden." We all lean in closer to see...a blinking jewel in a piece of stone that also has some sort of old symbol-laden language carved into it.

"So, where is he?" I ask.

"Well..." Ford frowns and picks up the tablet. "I'm still working on deciphering that. This was created long before man had a full understanding of world geography, but in theory, I should be able to overlay this against a modern map and once that's done have fairly accurate coordinates."

"How long?" Roar demands, cutting to the chase.

"I'm close," Ford hedges.

"Ha!" Roar laughs. "That means two moons."

"A week, it means a week!" Ford corrects. "It meant two moons back before the internet. Now...a week."

We're all quiet. Finally, I say as gently as I can, "We don't have that long."

Helena stands. "He'll have it by tomorrow."

Ford blinks at her. "I will?"

She gives him one of her shark smiles. "I'll be your motivation."

Ford swallows. Hard. "Tomorrow is doable."

Aden knocks his fists against the table, calling our attention his way. "And Maddie will motivate me to find a doorway into the hideaway from below."

Maddie gives her head a little shake. "He means if we know where it is, he can get us in through Hades. Which is easy for him and requires no extra motivation."

"But you will give it anyway," Aden says in a low voice.

Maddie laughs and leans close to whisper something to him that from Aden's reaction does not seem like a refusal.

"And I will go with Crystal and protect her in case all of you fail, which seems most likely," Roar announces.

I glare at him. "Roar, don't be a buzzkill."

He snorts. "I have not killed any buzzes."

"You did," I tell him and then push him into a chair. It's my turn to speak. "This is going to sound crazy, but what if we just give Busk the last piece and let him use it and fry himself with it the way that Bobby did?"

Helena opens her mouth like she's about to tell me I'm an idiot, but then a look of consideration crosses her face and she closes it again.

"That's interesting," Ford says with his professor look on his face and I almost beam with pride. "I think we should still assume the worst would occur, but let me check on that. I need my laptop..."

He rushes out of the room. Helena shakes her head. "That's his research hard-on. It's almost as impressive as his—"

Maddie interrupts. "I have an idea to go along with Crystal's. He wants to use her to find the last piece, which he is too dumb to realize is already right under his nose. What if we let him think he's found that piece?"

"A magical duplicate?" Aden grins at Maddie. "That is your specialty."

Maddie nods, looking excited and also a little scared. "I've never tried to duplicate anything other than myself...but I think that I could if I tried."

"I know exactly what it looks like," I say. "I could sketch it out. Would that help?"

"Immensely." She turns to rummage in a drawer behind her and comes back with a pack of colored pencils and some paper.

"While you draw, I'll bake a cake," Maddie says. "Just in case it is your birthday."

Helena stands. "And I am going to grab a bottle of champagne from my cellar. We're going to do a toast to taking down Busk—no matter what it takes."

My hand trembles a bit at this and the line I'd been carefully drawing smudges. I agree we need to take Busk down

—but I refuse to let sacrificing Harmony be part of what it takes.

My head hits the table with a resounding thud, the reverberation spreading through my skull into what promises to become a banger of a headache. But right now, I don't care. It can't be any worse than the one I've already got; a headache that the son of the underworld, two newly-minted goddesses, the world's greatest lover, and a berserker can't come up with a solution to.

Then how the hell am I going to?

9

____

While the cake bakes we hobble together the rough version of a plan. Okay, it's seat of our pants and depends on ten different things going right—starting with Ford figuring out his magical tracking signal. But at least it's better than nothing.

Then, while we wait for it to cool, Maddie and Helena try to help me tap into my power. They tried their best, but mostly they just told me to reach deep inside and let it out. Which… didn't work.

"Maybe today isn't my birthday after all," I say to them.

"Have you had any other indications of your powers coming in?" Maddie asks. "Other than what happened earlier?"

Blushing, I shake my head. Maddie's powers had come on without her even meaning to, and Helena had been blocking hers with magical suppressant pills, and she'd still grown horns overnight. Me, the girl who's been surrounded by magic and spells since birth, hasn't even blipped a bloop on the magical Richter scale.

"No," I admit. "I mean, there was this one time with a toilet—"

"It's a bidet," Helena interrupts me. "And that was my apartment. There was nothing magical about it, except for the fact that you had gone your whole life without knowing what one was."

"Regardless," Maddie steps in. "Your powers not coming in are actually to our benefit. If you're not giving off any signals, then Busk can't track you."

"Yeah, I guess," I say, still sniffling. "But it's still embarrassing to be the magical virgin in the room, I mean, at least with my own powers."

Maddie disagrees. "Oh, but think of all the options. You're a water sign, right? You might be able to stop tsunamis from taking out entire cities!"

"Or you could cause them," says Helena, caustically.

"I'm a Gemini, the twins. So I can split myself," Maddie continues. "Helena is a Capricorn, a sea goat."

"And a sexy one," Ford comes in to grab some water and as he walks by tugs on Helena's updo to reveal her curled horns, which look like marble.

"I'm a Cancer," I chime in. "The crab."

Everyone sits quietly for a second with that one.

"Maybe you'll develop really great hand strength," Maddie says helpfully, mimicking pincers.

"Or maybe your eyes will grow on stalks," Helena says, and Ford gives her a little pat that probably is their couple's signal to pipe down. He whispers in her ear, "behave" before heading back to his research in the other room.

"Okay, great," I say, my lip starting to tremble again. "Harmony is in danger, and my powers could come in as anything from weird eye formations to a powerful STD. Awesome."

Roar stands resolutely, his chest puffing out. "I will protect you from STDs."

"I have to go," I say, pushing back from the table a little unsteadily. "I appreciate you guys wanting to throw a little party, but I can't sit here and eat cake while Harmony is being held by Busk." I ball my fists. "It's time to woman-up."

Roar stands. "Then I will go with you. A woman should not woman-up without a man."

"Okay, look," I say, spinning on him. "I will allow you to come with me, but you've got to stop being sexist."

"I'm afraid I cannot," Roar says, and I catch him checking himself out in the hallway mirror.

"Sexist," I correct him. "Not sexy. And being sexist is not sexy."

"It's really not," Ford agrees as he returns once more, this time with a sheaf of papers in his hands. "I've found a little clarity on the question of whether the *talentum* will take out Busk like it did your husband.

"Bobby," I say, at the same time that Maddie whispers "Bert" and Helena mutters, "Robert."

"Yeah, that guy," Ford confirms. "I'd been doing some research before Helena found her powers, trying to better understand the proving yourself worthy clause."

"Oh that thing," I say, "I'd forgotten all about that."

"Really?" Helena stares at me. "Haven't you been at all concerned that it won't find you worthy and that the *talentum* will end you?"

"Not really." I shrug. "I figured if I approach my powers with an open heart that it will all work out."

Helena rolls her eyes. "Of course you didn't stress about it."

Maddie nudges her. "That's a good thing, Helena. She doesn't need to get herself all knotted up about being the *talentum*'s top of class; she has enough on her plate."

"I just don't understand that type of thinking," Helena admits.

"We know," I say, and I give her a quick little hug. "Your uber intensity is why we love you."

"Same," Ford agrees, "And as much as I love this bonding moment you ladies are having, can we get back to my discovery?"

"Is it good news?" I ask.

Ford scrunches up his face, "Any additional knowledge is helpful, so in that sense it's very good—"

"It's not good news," Helena interrupts. "Baby, don't sugar-coat it, just spit it out."

Ford sighs. "One who seeks the *talentum*'s powers must acquire its pieces via battle, sacrifice, or quest. I'm guessing

Robert did none of those?"

"No," Maddie confirms. "He paid cash."

"Or bartered," Helena adds.

"Or charmed," I say.

"But Busk did battle Maddie and me for her piece," Aden says.

"And I hurt him pretty bad," Helena says, "Which could count as sacrifice."

"So our fighting back actually helped him?" Maddie asks, looking a little green.

"What we're saying," I clarify, "Is that there is no way to depend on the *talentum* finding Busk unworthy?"

"How is that fair?" Maddie asks.

"The *talentum* is power," Roar says. "It doesn't care about fair. It wants to find someone powerful and unrelenting to wield its power."

"That makes no sense!" I throw my hands up. "Why would it choose the three of us then?"

Nobody says anything for a long moment.

Finally, Maddie speaks. "We're not powerful in the way that Busk is. He's all about swinging around his wangdoodle to prove what a big man he is. Our power comes from deeper inside."

"And that's how we'll take him down," Helena says, downing the last of her coffee. "But first we need to get you inside with Busk. I think you need some sort of protection—more than just that hunk of beefsteak beside you."

"Do not speak of Velvet Thunder in that way," Roar says. "I will allow no one to eat my stallion."

"I wasn't talking about the horse," she shoots back, and it looks like they're about to go full-on goddess vs. berserker. "We should arm Crystal to the teeth with magical dongles and stuff."

"Stop!" I shout, throwing my hands in the air. "Helena, I appreciate it, but any magical object I try to take in will probably just be confiscated by Busk."

"I don't like it, either," Maddie says. "But she's right. We have to trust Crystal to go in alone."

"I won't be totally alone," I tell them. "Harmony and communicated on the astral plane last night. I'm hoping since we made that connection that we'll be able to speak telepathically when we're physically near one another. Busk doesn't know, and it's an ace up my sleeve." Something occurs to me and I look at the two of them. "You know, the three of us have a strong connection too; maybe we could communicate the same way."

Maddie immediately shakes her head. "I'm not really interested in having my spirit leave my body. Especially when you told me that there's a danger of never finding my way back."

"Same," Helena agrees. "Let's stick to texting."

"You guys..." It's rare that I'm the exasperated one, but honestly sometimes I get sick of being treated like I don't have a clue. "We wouldn't need to go all the way to the astral plane, we could just kinda mentally connect, sorta like ESP, but it's a three-way channel for just the three of us."

Maddie and Helena exchange doubtful glances.

"We're already clutching at straws," I remind them. "What's one more?"

"You have a point," Helena concedes and from her this is actually a huge concession.

Grinning, I clap my hands. "It helps to have some sort of physical connection, and the easiest way to do that is with hair." Actually if I hadn't already drank my entire thermos of panda dung tea, that would also work, but it's probably just as well it's gone, because I have a feeling the name would've been a turn off for them. My second option, though, should work just as well.

I grab scissors out of Maddie's knife block. Even as she protests that those are only for food, I snip two long strands of hair from my red curls. "Now you guys do the same and we can each braid the other's hair into our own."

Helena takes the scissors from me. "I knew you'd eventually have us braiding each other's hair; I just didn't know this is how it would go down."

Maddie cuts her hair last and then we all take turns braiding the strands into one another's hair...and yes, Helena is right, this is just the type of sisterhood I always dreamed of us having. The only thing that could possibly make it better was if we were all singing, "We Are Family."

Well, that and if Busk wasn't holding my mother hostage and threatening the safety of the entire world.

10

———

Everyone seems impressed by my resolve, and it would be great to make a dramatic exit right now... except I rode a horse here and the address Busk texted me isn't really within cantering distance.

Aden must be following my thoughts, because he throws me a key. "Take my bike. I had a witch magic it so I always get green lights and cops can't clock the speed with their radar."

"Thank you," I say, looking at the familiar Harley logo shining brightly in my palm.

"Please, leave Velvet Thunder tied up. He will be happy eating your lawn. If you let him roam free he will come to find me. I want him to remain safe. Also, do not allow this insane person to eat him," Roar finishes, nodding at Helena.

My heart melts a little at Roar's love for his steed. He's such an alpha, but every once in a while I can see the cracks. He has genuine emotions and real love in his heart...for his horse, anyway. And he's made it very clear that the *talentum* is his main focus in this whole mess, so I need to keep my head on straight.

I can't have my thoughts filled with Roar. His are on the *talentum*...and Velvet Thunder. I need to be worried about Harmony—and only her.

I look at my sister-wives...no. Our bond is stronger than just that we were married to the same man. We're friends now. Real, honest, chosen friends.

"I'm scared," I admit.

"We were too," Helena says, which is a shocking thing to hear her admit.

"We have your back," Maddie confirms. "As soon as you need us, we're there."

Roar and I head outside, where he rubs noses with Velvet for a minute before coming to Aden's motorcycle, which he eyes apprehensively.

"I don't know how to ride," he admits.

I want to laugh, he looks like a little boy; there's even a blush rising in his cheeks. "I used to have a motorcycle," I tell him. "A little thing, not like this. But I know how to ride. Get on the back."

I thought he'd protest at riding "bitch," but he doesn't. I once had a boyfriend throw a fit when I tried to put him on the back of my Vespa. I'd flipped him the bird and left him choking on my exhaust. I expect Roar to be equally put out, but either he took my comment about sexism seriously, or he realizes that real men aren't upset by such things.

The big lug refuses to wear a helmet, until I go back inside, grab a tomato off Maddie's counter, then throw it on the road, stomping on the gooey remains to drive my point home. He puts it on, but is definitely sulking as we speed away.

His grip is light on my waist, like he's resisting the touch of my skin, but I take the first turn pretty tight and he has to hold on for dear life. The truth is I'm not used to his bulk on the back of the bike, but if he wants to believe that was a power move on my part, I'll take it.

I got rid of my own bike after Harmony told me she saw my life being changed by one. I had imagined hospital beds, feeding tubes and wheelchairs, but as Roar leans into me something deep inside responds to his touch, I realize the only danger here isn't to my body—it's my heart that's going to be forever changed.

The address that Busk gave me is on the water, but it's not an abandoned dock or a derelict wharf. After feeding Bobby to the Jersey Hydra, I'd just about written off going anywhere near the docks again—and it wasn't just murder that made me feel that way. Everything about it had felt bad, from the smell to the cracked pavement in the parking lot.

But Busk is the richest man on earth, and it looks like he's acquired an entire stretch of beach just for himself, then turned it into nature's playground. Everywhere I look are green growing things. Everything is immaculately land-scaped, but it can't hide the fact that there's razor wire at the top of the fence, and a guard tower at the entrance.

I roll up, and flip up the visor to my helmet. "I'm Crystal Sky. Geoff Busk is expecting me."

The guard looks at me and then at Roar. "Only you," he tells me.

Roar tears his helmet off and jumps away from the bike, ready to pop every limb this guy has right out of their sockets.

"Being sexist isn't sexy," he says sternly to the guard, who looks at me with confusion.

"This isn't sexism, Roar," I explain, but his eyes have started to go milky. I don't need him to go full on berserker. I hop off the bike, and get in between them.

"This guy is just doing his job," I tell Roar. "He's probably not even that evil."

"I'm not evil," the guard agrees. "I lost my job at the plant and found this one online. It doesn't even pay that great. If you wanna go in, I'm not going to die over it."

Roar nods and puts a hand on the man's shoulder. "Thank you, coward man. I am glad I did not have to kill you."

The guard glances in between us, then reaches into the kiosk and opens the gate. "There's an access building, straight ahead. You can't miss it."

"I miss nothing," Roar says stiffly, stalking forward. I hurry to catch up to him, and we follow the mulched path as greenery closes around us. Sprays of water shoot out intermittently, and my hand wanders to find Roar's. This would all be extremely pleasant if I didn't know it was the secret lair of a global villain.

We come to the access building the guard mentioned. It's a brick shed with a single door. Roar yanks the door open to reveal an elevator. He turns to me with a question in his eyes, but all I can do is shrug—what choice do we have?

There's only one way to go, and that's down. I push the button and it dings, filling the room with elevator music.

"This is so weird..." I mutter as we step inside.

Roar nods and flexes his muscles. "I will defend you with my life."

Me? Or the *talentum*? I want to ask, but the elevator has a camera, and I'm sure it's bugged, too. Busk already knows we're coming; he doesn't need to know what's inside my heart, too.

I'm so distracted that I don't see Busk—or the rifle he's holding.

Until he points it at Roar's chest and pulls the trigger.

11

───────

I've never been athletic, or fast, but I swear I could have thrown myself in front of the shot aimed at Roar. And maybe I did, in my mind or in my heart, but in the real world—where it actually matters—all I can do is turn and stare, gaping as I expect his chest to break open, and all of his lifeblood to come out.

Instead, a dart sticks out of his chest.

"What...?" I ask as he reaches for it and pulls it out.

"Do you think that a puny bug bite like this will bring me down?" he roars, flicking it aside with a smirk "I am a berserker—and you're about to fully understand what that means."

His face gets red...but his eyes don't change. They don't cloud over with the whites that mean he has entered his berserking stage. Confusion clouds his face, as his jaw muscles twitch.

"I don't…I don't understand…" His rage fizzles. He drops to his knees and I kneel beside him.

"Roar? Are you hurt?" I ask desperately, clawing around on the floor to find the dart. "Did you poison him, you son of bitch?" I yell at Busk.

Busk lowers his rifle. "Don't be dramatic. It's just a little serum I had my R&D guys cook up."

"What did you do to him?" I shout, desperately searching Roar's body for any ill effects. But he just looks…normal. Except for the sheen of helplessness spreading over his face and the absolute sadness that is deepening in his eyes.

"You were supposed to come alone," Busk says, casually handing the rifle over to a goon that has come to his side. "Certainly not with a Viking berserker. But women never listen, so I was prepared. I thought you might bring the lawyer bitch, or maybe the hot housewife. That dart was full of an experimental anti-magic serum. I didn't know how much effect it might have on your goddess friends. But your"—he flicks his fingers at Roar, clearly unimpressed by him.—"whatever he is to you…is fully human now."

"You can't do that to him!" I shout, my hands pressing at the spot on Roar's shirt where I can see a small drop of blood. Now I understand the despair in his eyes, the tight grip Roar has on my wrist. His power, his identity—it's all wrapped up in being a berserker. Without that, he won't know how to be…or even who he is.

"Human?" Roar looks like he was just pronounced with a death sentence. He howls in frustration, clawing at his chest, pushing my hands away.

"Roar, it's okay," I whisper to him. "It's not that bad. You'll just have to eat more protein, and probably start using conditioner if you want to retain your luxurious—"

"Human!!?!" he cries out again, his fingers going to his own throat, as if he wants to choke himself."

"Well, so am I," I say, starting to be a little offended. "It's not that bad."

"You cannot begin to understand," he tells me.

I know people think I'm stupid, but I'm truly not. Busk had said the serum is experimental, which means it's not a hundred percent tested, and probably not FDA approved, either. The truth is that Roar might think I might not fully understand what just happened, but Busk probably doesn't either. This serum might be effective for twenty minutes, it might be twenty days. Or...it might be forever.

"How long does it last?" I ask, turning to Busk.

"Forever," he says, but I see his eye twitch. He has no idea.

I lean into Roar, pulling his hands from his throat. "I need you. We will reverse this, but right now, I need you," I repeat. Even if he is *just* human now, he's the only friend I have here.

Roar looks at me with those blue piercing eyes. He stands and sweeps me under his arm, giving me a squeeze. Berserker or not, he's built like a brick shithouse. I hug Roar back.

"You're impressive even when you're human," I reassure him. "I like you this way just as much."

"Wait until I start to menstruate," he says stiffly.

"Oh honey, that's not how that works," I say.

"If you're done cuddling—" Busk starts, and I come to my feet.

"No, you're the one that's done," I tell him. "Actually, no—I am. I'm done with you. I didn't come here for the rainforest tour and undersea adventure. I came here for Harmony. Now take me to her."

Of course it's not that easy. First Busk has his goons take us into a room where we have to strip down and are thoroughly inspected for contraband. It's probably best that Roar doesn't have his berserker abilities right now, 'cause I don't think he would've made it through the moment he's told to bend over and cough.

The whole ordeal is humiliating, but I remind myself that my body is just a vessel and it doesn't define me. The worst part is that I insist that I have nothing on me and then the amulet I used yesterday to speak with Harmony, falls out of my bra. I forgot that I tucked it back in there this morning after my shower, figuring it couldn't hurt. Now that I think about it, that's probably what gave me the power over that morning dew. My *talentum* powers are starting to emerge and the amulet must've let me access them in a moment of high emotion. It's too late to do anything with that now, the guard tucks it away and I'm pretty sure that's the last time I'll ever see it.

Once we're both cleared, Busk gives us different clothes—sort of a mix between what you'd wear at a high-end spa that also operates as a prison. It seems like the worst is over, but right before the door opens, two goons cover our heads with cloth hoods.

"Hey!" I protest. And I can hear a fight going on that I'm pretty sure is Roar. It lasts a while so it must take a few goons to subdue him.

"Just knock him out," I hear Busk yell, sounding impatient.

"No!" I yell. But it's too late—a moment later I hear a grunt and then a ground shaking thump that can only be Roar hitting the floor.

"Come, my dear." Busk's oily voice is in my ear and his hand on my elbow, steering me forward. Being blinded and at the mercy of a madman is not a great combo, but Roar already proved that there's no point in struggling.

We walk a few feet before Busk speaks again, "Your chariot awaits." To the goons he says, "Throw the Viking in the back."

I get into some sort of vehicle. From the sound of the high-pitched engine, it's small, maybe even a golf cart. We drive for a long while and I try to pretend I'm scratching my face while really making a move to pull my hood off. But Busk is by my side and immediately gives my hand a little swat.

"No, no, no," He tsks. Then he grabs both of my hands in his clammy ones and holds them tight until the vehicle finally comes to a stop.

Once again, Busk directs me off my seat and then we walk several feet before I hear a door open. The hood comes off and I'm shoved into a room, so bright that I'm momentarily blinded.

Harmony doesn't belong in a cage, even if that prison is surrounded by water. She's facing the glass, and some fish have congregated to her, all of them wiggling to try to get close to the finger she has pressed against the glass.

"Mom!" I cry when I see her, falling forward into her arms.

"Stop with that," Harmony says, patting my hair. "You know I love you; we don't need to use the normal worlds that everyone else does. Also—"

She pushes me away from her, holding my shoulder at arm's length. "Why in the holy fucking hell are you here? I told you three different ways not to do this, you stupid, stupid girl."

"Nice family," Busk says from the door, his goon still at his elbow.

"At least I've got one," I shoot back. I wouldn't normally stoop to such a low blow, but I'm pretty sure Busk isn't the sensitive type and also in countless interviews he's bragged about how he believes that his lone wolf status is part why he's become so powerful. Surprisingly though, I see his eye twitch again. Huh...does the world's worst person have a weak spot? I tuck that little bit away in case it might come in handy later.

"The women need their time," Roar says sternly. "You must give them privacy before letting the old one go."

"Excuse me?" Harmony asks, snapping her eyes to him.

"Did you really think I would just let her go?" Busk asks, his gaze sweeping Roar as he approaches him. Even without his berserker magic, he's an intimidating mountain of muscle. Busk takes a step backward, and his minion comes forward, swinging his rifle around. Even so, Roar doesn't stop until the muzzle is snug against his chest.

"Harmony has an ability like I've never seen."

"What did you do?" I ask her, raising my eyebrows.

She shrugs, and rolls her eyes. "A few small curses."

"Harmony!" I exclaim. "Curses are bad juju!"

"Crystal, open your eyes!" She sweeps her arm around, indicating Busk, the goons, and her cell. "Bad juju is the least of our worries right now."

There's no point in arguing with Harmony; she always twists things so she's right. But no matter what kind of deep doodoo we might be in, there's no call to add bad juju to it. Harmony has told me more than once that the evil you put out into the world always comes back to you.

"What was the curse?" I ask.

"Boils," Busk says, sounding cheerful in a way that tells me he wasn't affected.

Harmony gives him a sour look. "That's right. And I warned them when they entered my house. Any part of them that touches any part of me will be covered in boils before the sun crosses the horizon."

Busk laughs. "My guys didn't even know what boils were...at least not until they found their hands and arms covered in them. One guy even had them on his tongue."

"He licked me," Harmony adds in a flat voice.

"He did!" Busk chuckles. "The sicko! You always get one or two freaks in any batch of hired muscle. Some try to weed them out, but I like the excitement they add."

"Well, I hope you aren't thinking of recruiting Harmony. She would never work for you!"

"Yes, Crystal, he and I have already discussed that. For goddess' sake, did you just come here to state the obvious?"

"Harmony…" I start, hurt, but Busk cuts me off.

"I like collecting magical objects, and magical humans too. Most of them choose to work for me, eventually, after some convincing. Some just want money. I have plenty of that. But some require other methods. I think your mother and I will come to terms; she just needs some more time here to think about it."

Even though I suspected all along that Busk would never let Harmony go, I hate that he wants to keep her forever. Like she's some sort of pet. And I've already seen how he treats his magical employees. He had witches at Maddie's wedding whose entire job was just to heal him. Never mind that healing takes tons of a witch's' energy and can even kill them if they overdue it. I can't see that being the type of thing that would bother Busk. I'm sure he sees them as replaceable, just like his goons.

"I've got a date with destiny," Busk says, nearly clicking his heels. "But this human"—he hits on the word particularly hard, giving Roar a dismissive glance—"has a point. You do deserve the chance to hug it out with mom. And I want you ladies to enjoy the next hour, because after that, things are going to become very unpleasant."

I straighten my shoulders and stare him down. I knew he'd keep Harmony. I knew he'd try to find a way to make me talk. What I didn't know was how scared I'd be.

"I told you," I say. "I don't know where it is."

"You said that, yes," Busk says, reaching out to tuck a piece of hair behind my ear. He leans in closer, his breath tickling my neck. Roar growls, a low, aggressive sound that bounces off the glass walls.

"Unfortunately for you, dear Crystal," Busk whispers, "I don't believe you."

12

—————

"What were you thinking?" Harmony practically screeches at me once Busk has gone and the door has closed behind us. "I told you not to come here. Why don't you ever listen to me?"

There's a flare of anger in my gut, something I wasn't expecting. Yes, I knew Harmony would be mad at me for disobeying her, but also, I'm a grown-ass woman—and it's time to show her exactly that.

"Why don't I listen to you?" I shoot back. "Because sometimes you're wrong. Has that ever occurred to you?"

Harmony's jaw clicks shut and she stares at me in surprise. I push the anger down and reach out to her spirit. Busk might have made a big deal out of leaving us alone to have some privacy before he puts us through whatever hell comes next, but I'd bet my fancy days-of-the-week underwear that we're under surveillance right now. For all I know the fish outside the glass are actually robots.

Harmony, I close my eyes, stretching my consciousness towards her. Instead of leaving my body and entering the astral plane, instead it's like I can feel my words splitting the air between us as they travel toward Harmony.

What? she shoots back, still ticked. But then her expression turns to one of surprise. *Crystal, how did you learn telepathy overnight?*

I didn't, I send the thought her way, enjoying how easy it is to do. I'd thought there'd be more straining, but this is just as easy as talking aloud. *I think going to the astral plane kick-started it and I also drank a ton of your panda dung tea.*

MY SPECIAL TEA! That's for special use only! Her scolding tone makes me grit my teeth in annoyance.

Rescuing you is a special use!

Rescue! Harmony scoffs. *More like you got yourself captured along with me.*

I knew he wouldn't let you go. Stop assuming the worst. Stop always thinking that I'm dumb, or I don't know what I'm doing.

You don't know what you're doing, she insists. *Now he's got you, me, this living monument to pectoral muscles, and the* talentum.

But he doesn't know he has it.

He'll get you to talk. Harmony says. *I haven't been here long, but I've heard screams. He's not a man, he's a monster. And he will get what he wants come hell or high water.*

He doesn't know you're wearing the talentum. "We were strip searched," I say aloud.

"It was very unpleasant," Roar agrees.

How are you just in your normal clothes? I ask. *How do you still have the* talentum?

Harmony offers a smile. *Women my age are often overlooked. It's like we don't even exist.*

Well, that is one win in our column. Plus Busk doesn't know that we have our own method of communication.

So you came here so we could have a chat? The wave of sarcasm nearly scorches my brain.

No, of course not! I mentally snap back at her. *We came up with a plan to take down Busk.*

Really? Harmony does not sound impressed. *I've been gone less than twenty-four hours, so this must be some sort of last-minute plan you cobbled together with your friends—the ladies playing at being goddesses.*

What the Hades! I cry with enough mental fire to make Harmony wince. *Now you don't approve of my friends either? Is anything I do good enough for you?*

Turning away from Harmony, I break the mental connection.

Roar puts a hand on my shoulder. "Does your head ache? You were making strange faces a moment ago."

"My mother makes my head ache," I tell him.

"Imagine how I feel," Harmony mutters from behind me.

Directing my words to Roar, but with sentiments aimed at Harmony, I continue, "She is so stubborn that she can't listen to me for two seconds." I want to be strong, but despite myself tears fill my eyes. "She can't even consider that my coming here wasn't stupid, but instead an act of bravery...and love."

"Bravery can be stupid," Harmony shouts from behind me, no longer pretending this conversation isn't between us. "And love is the stupidest thing ever invented."

I spin around to face her. "Well, did you ever think that your love for me is maybe making you the stupid one?"

"Yes! I did! It probably is!" Harmony yells back at me. "I know you're capable of great things, but I'm scared of seeing you get hurt. Or worse—losing you!"

I stare at Harmony, who despite her harsh tone just said the words I've been wanting to hear for what feels like my whole life. "Okay," I say with a tentative smile, and then reach my hands out to her. "I don't want you to get hurt or to lose you either. So let's work together. Okay?"

After a long moment of hesitation, Harmony puts her hands in mine. *Okay,* she says her voice in my head once more. *What's the first part of this plan?*

We need Hepatitis.

Oh good lord. Harmony gives a shake of her head. *I suppose some of these goons must be carrying it, but I don't know how many of them you'd have to bone before catching the STD that you want.*

No! I mentally cry. *I don't want an STD. I want Hepatitis the person. She actually mostly goes by Hepa and I guess now I understand why. She's a tech witch who works for Nico. I'm sure if we combine our efforts we can reach out to her and make contact.*

What I feel next is pure doubt, along with indecision. My irritation rises.

Have some faith in me for once! I practically shout, and Harmony winces.

She relaxes, and I feel her consciousness moving toward mine. I relax, willing my negativity away as our deep selves combine, then push outward, sending psychic feelers into the universe. I picture Hepa, sitting behind her wall of computers, a permanent line between her eyebrows from either just being a constant bitch, or possibly screen time.

Hello?

Hepa! I call out. *It's me, Crystal!*

I don't know anyone named Bill, and you can eff right the hell off. Don't you know how rude it is to just show up in someone's subconscious? If you try to mindmeld me a dick pic, I'll wither it before you can throw up a penis protection sp—

IT'S CRYSTAL! NOT BILL! I shout as loudly as I can with my mental voice.

Harmony's mouth twitches as she tries to strengthen the connection. I might have been able to find Hepa, but she's not a psychic, only a witch, and we don't have a strong bond. The signal is weak, and I can only hope she has the information I need.

Crystal the human? Oh right, Nico said you'd be calling. I was only half-listening to him, though, so I must've missed the part where he said you wouldn't be using a telephone.

Yes, I say. *Busk has us, me and my mother Harmony. He doesn't know it, but the third piece of the* talentum *is here, too. Harmony is wearing it. She's masking it with a spell for now, but it won't be long until he breaks it—or one of us.*

Why...the fuck...asshole?

Hepa is breaking up, so I stop trying to send words. Instead I send her a mental image of being blindfolded, put into a vehicle, and driven to this cell that is probably underwater. Hopefully this can help Ford better pinpoint our location. What I get in response is a quick rap, one time.

Once for yes, Harmony tells me. *She's using old-school table rapping.*

Our signal is fading, so I hurry to the next question. *Was Maddie able to make the copy of the third piece?*

The silence lasts for so long that I think the connection might've been lost, but finally she gives one knock in response.

My knees go weak with relief. Maddie did it! When Busk comes back to question me, I can hold out for a bit and then direct him to the fake. Hopefully that will buy us enough time for everything else.

Now's the tougher question, and it's not a yes or no. *Where did she hide it?*

The wharf...where it all...began...

The sound might be able to travel to me, but I don't think Hepa can hold on much longer, or communicate much more.

Technically I've gotten all that I need from her, but I have one last idea that I didn't share with anyone else.

Gathering all my strength I send her another image—the *talentum* on fire, golden ring melting into a puddle, magic pouring out of it, burning up, evaporating into smoke. I send her a picture of me destroying my third of the most powerful magic object on earth, and the one thing that could make me a goddess.

HOW? I ask, pushing the one word out with all my might.

Crystal! Harmony is shocked. Her tether on the communication with Hepa snaps, but not before I hear a single knock in response. Hepa heard me. She understands.

Unfortunately, so does Harmony.

No! She's seething, her eyes meeting mine. *The* talentum *will never forgive you, Crystal. It will kill you!*

Yeah, she might. But I don't admit this out loud or even mentally. I keep it as a very tiny thought tucked deep, deep inside of me. Because it's not like I want to die. Or disappoint the goddess. And I was actually looking super forward to having cool lady powers along with Maddie and Helena. Even if the goddess doesn't kill me, I'll be the lame human while my two friends are ruling dirt and air.

But I don't really have a choice. As long as the *talentum* exists, Busk can have that power, too. It's not worth it. I cede my share. I give up my chance. I won't risk the world for my own sake.

How? I demand of Hepa once more. I have to force the one word out alone, because Harmony wrenches her hands from my own.

Distantly I hear Hepa reply, *Salt*—and then the connection is gone. I'm not even certain if I heard her correctly, because blood is rushing through my ears and the room has started to wobble around me. I try to reach out, reestablish the connection, but there's nothing left in me.

I fall forward onto my knees. Roar catches me, his strong arms lowering me to the floor. The last thing I see is Harmony hovering over me, her finger twisting the *talentum* on her finger in worry.

13

———

Apparently any quality family time that Busk intends to give us also comes with an armed guard. I don't believe for one second that we aren't under constant surveillance, but when I come around in Roar's arms—waking up there is becoming a habit—there's a man with a gun standing with his back against the door.

"Crystal!" Harmony is snapping her fingers in front of my nose, a stern look on her face. "What have I told you about sugar intake? You always do this; eat for comfort and then collapse when the sugar burns off!"

"Wha???" I ask, my head still fuzzy from the psychic messaging overload with Hepa.

"It'll pass," Harmony says to the guard, including him in the conversation. "But you should've seen her as a teenager. She found a lot of comfort in the Little Debbie aisle."

She holds her arms out in front of her stomach and I hear a deep rumble coming from Roar. "Women are beautiful at any size," he says. "I would comfort any of them, and be grateful."

"Nice body positivity," I tell him, then pull his head down to mine. "She's covering for me," I whisper. "We can't have Busk figure out that we're psychically communicating with the outside world."

"You were not large once?" Roar asks, his eyes roaming down my decidedly trim torso.

"Not even close," I tell him. "Harmony won't have processed foods in the house. I grew up on sticks and lettuce."

"You grew well," he says solemnly.

"Ehhh…" The guard eyes me, holding his palm out and wobbling it side to side. "She's a Jersey six."

"Excuse me!" I say, bolting to my feet, despite the shakiness in my legs.

"Don't get all bent out of shape, babe," the guy goes on. "You're just not my type. I like a little more meat on the bone."

I toss my hair, temper still fired. "Attracting you, or caring what you think of my appearance, is the last thing I'm worried about," I inform him. "That you would rate women on sight, with absolutely no appreciation for their inner spirit, is what I find despicable."

"Tell that to my wife," he says, his face suddenly sad. "She hit thirty and got all worried about her body, working out all the time, eating like a rabbit. It's that phone is what it is. She started watching all these videos about keeping your skin tight, your boobs in the right place. Now I can't hardly find her under the face cream at night. And you know how you mark a kid's height against the wall with the dates?"

Harmony and I both nod.

"Now we've got one with where her boobs are at. She's checking to make sure they don't drop."

"This is your job," Roar says accusingly, pointing his finger at the man.

"I tell her all the time—they're still in the same place. Well, the left one is, anyway."

"No," Roar shakes his head. "You make her feel like she has to do this. It is not the phone. It is her man that has made her feel inadequate."

The man looks at me, a sudden well of sadness in his eyes. It opens up a pit in my stomach, one that drops all of my concerns, our entire situation, out of consideration. There is a human in front of me that is hurting; I might be able to fix that.

"What's your name?" I ask the guard, moving toward him.

"Frank," he says, breaking my gaze to glance down at his gun.

"Well, Frank." I lean against the wall next to him, letting our shoulders touch. "When was the last time you talked to your wife about this?"

"Last night," he says, promptly.

"And what did you say?"

"Left one's still a bit lower, baby."

Harmony sighs and puts her head in her hands, but I signal to her to be quiet. "No, I mean like really talked to her. Have you told her that you love her for who she is, not what she looks like?"

"Of course I..." Frank starts out irate, ready to defend his husband skills, but then his eyes go a little vacant.

"Fraaaaank," Harmony chides. "Be honest. This woman would be better off without you, wouldn't she?"

"Harmony!" I snap at her.

"What?" She demands. "99.9 percent of the time it's true. Men need women. Women also need women. Nobody needs men."

"Hey, two girls can't make a baby together," Frank cuts in. I'd tell him not to bother going down this path, because I already know Harmony's answer. It's not that she raised me to be a man-hater. Not exactly. It was more of a 'men— what's the point even-er.'

Now, taking a step toward Frank with the scary look in her eye that she tends to get during these kinds of discussions, she explains, "Sure, you need a man to make a baby. You need him for what, 30 seconds, tops?"

"My seed takes much longer than that to empty," Roar offers.

"Yeah, um..." Frank gulps and takes a small step back. "Mine too."

I step in front of Harmony before she advances further into Frank's space.

"Don't listen to them," I tell Frank. "I believe your wife does need you. And for more than just measuring her boobs." His eyes, wide and confused, lock onto mine hopefully.

"You think?"

"Yes," I say, forcefully. And I believe it too. There's a goodness in Frank. It's more than just something I believe...it's almost like I can feel it. "Frank," I say now. "You tell her that you love her, don't you?"

"Every night," he says, straightening up and sticking his jaw out. "I tell Bethany that I love her every night."

"You should be showing her," Roar says, his accusing pointer finger coming back out. "You do not tell a woman you love her with your words, you show her by slaying her enemies."

"No, you don't slay her enemies unless she asks you to," I snap back at Roar. "That's because you treat her like a partner, not some damsel in distress."

"Um, I don't know that Bethany has many enemies," Frank says, clearly confused by this turn in the conversation.

I turn back to him. "Sorry, no, of course not." I send one last glare towards Roar over my shoulder, and then give Frank my full attention. "I know what we're going to do. Frank, lie down here on the floor next to me."

"What?" He asks, his eyebrows flying up to his—admittedly —receding hairline.

I lie down in the middle of the room, and extend a hand to him. "We're role playing," I explain. "I'm your wife. Her name is Bethany?"

"Role playing," Roar nods solemnly. "I know this thing. It is good. Frank, lie down with the woman. Pretend she is your wife...to a point. If you touch her I will have to break your fingers."

"Roar! You are not breaking his fingers and Frank is going to be a gentleman, right, Frank?"

Frank shoots a nervous glance Roar's way, gulps, and then nods. "Perfectly perfect gentleman," he agrees. "But ugh, I'm not sure about the lying down part." He glances surreptitiously at the plant in the corner. Harmony follows his gaze and moves her body to block what is undoubtedly a hidden camera.

"Better?" she asks, folding her arms in a way that tells me she's going along with this right now, but is going to give me an earful later. Great.

"Alright," Frank says, edging toward me. "What do I do?"

"C'mere," I say, and pull him down next to me. Frank awkwardly falls to his knees, then gives Roar a look. "Look, I know your powers are off, but if you try anything..." He rubs his finger along the barrel of the gun, and I see the Viking start to puff his chest out.

"Nobody's trying anything, Frank," I assure him. "This isn't a trick, or anything like that. This is all about you, and fixing whatever is going on with your wife."

I make eye contact with Roar as I say this, hoping he'll understand that I really do mean it. A muscle flickers in his jawline and I can see he doesn't like it.

Finally, he gives a tight nod. "Okay...partner," he adds softly. Partner. My heart gives a foolish little pitter pat at this. Is it possible Roar really took in what I just said? And that he wants to be that type of partner...with me?

I want to chew on this information and decide how I feel about it, but first there's Frank and his love life. "Now what?" he asks as he lies next to me.

"First of all, you need to relax," Harmony says. She nods to Roar to switch places with her, and he comes to stand where she was, his broad shoulders blocking the hidden camera as she moves toward us.

"Let's get this over with," she says, standing at our heads. "How do you sleep with your wife?"

"Now hold on a minute, I'm not—" Frank moves to get up but Harmony grabs his shoulders and neatly pins him to the floor, her years of doing Reiki coming in useful as her grip strength immobilizes him.

"It's okay, Frank," I say, giving his hand a soft pat to make up for Harmony's rougher treatment. "She doesn't mean how you are with your wife in a sexual sense," I clarify. "Do you sleep touching? Holding hands? Do you spoon?"

"What's that got to do—"

"Frank, stop stalling!" Harmony bursts out.

"Harmony, stop pushing him so hard," I snap right back at her. "He's afraid."

"No, I'm not!" Frank protests, going red in the face.

But he is. I can feel the fear and it's not from being in a cell with three prisoners who might be dangerous. It's a fear of intimacy.

"Let's back up a little," I say to him, and Harmony sighs with annoyance.

"This is a waste of time," she says. "This goon probably thinks love is tattooing his wife's face on his arm."

Frank's hand goes to his right bicep. "Uh...that's wrong?"

"No, it's not," I say and then glare at Harmony until she takes a step back. "There is no right or wrong when it comes to love." I lie back on the hard floor again. "Now," I say, "how does your wife sleep? Back? Side?"

"On her side," Frank says.

"Like this?" I ask, rolling onto my side, facing him.

"No, facing the other way," he answers.

I flip the other way. "And then you spoon her?"

"Umm...not exactly." I can feel the fear welling up in Frank again.

Keeping my voice calm and soft, I say, "That's okay. Would she rest her head on your shoulder?"

"No, it's more like..." I look over my shoulder to see that Frank has gone red in the face.

"What do you need, Frank?" I ask. He clears his throat and steals a glance at Roar. "I feel like he's judging me."

Roar opens his mouth, no doubt to tell Frank he is being judged.

"Roar wouldn't judge you," I say loudly, "because Roar is not perfect. In fact, he would be terrified to be as honest as you're being right now."

Again, strangely, I know this is true. Roar is hiding a huge part of himself, deep away inside.

As if proving my words true, Roar's gaze skitters away from mine. "Your mother is right. We need to wrap this up. Another guard will be coming to find why the camera is blocked."

At this Frank jumps to his feet. I think it's over and that I've lost him, but instead he blurts out, "There's nothing to role play here. She sleeps on her side of the bed and I sleep on mine."

"And what's between you?" I ask, wanting to remind him their love bridges the gulf.

"Petunia our goldendoodle," Frank answers.

Roar groans and Harmony snickers.

Frank's eyes dart between the two of them. Wanting him to stop worrying about them, I stand directly in front of him.

"Look at me, Frank. Tell me when you stopped snuggling Bethany?" Harmony demands.

"Since always," he says. "Bethany says I snore."

"Snoring is what happens when a man has not emptied his —" Roar starts to say.

"Shut up with that," I cut him off. "You snore."

"Yes," he admits. "Because I have not emptied my—"

"Don't listen to him," I interject. "Snoring is not caused by sperm backup, and also, there are plenty of ways to address that. Now, you said you tell Bethany you love her every night? Show me."

I turn back around, looking away from Frank. A meaty hand clamps onto my shoulder. "Love ya, babe," he says.

"That's it?" Harmony asks.

"What?" Frank asks. "What's wrong with that?"

"To be honest, it makes me feel like a New Jersey zero," I tell him.

To his credit, Frank blushes. "Sorry about that six comment earlier," Frank says. "I'm sure for the right guy, you're a ten. It's just not me."

"Is Bethany your ten?" I ask him.

"Bethany's a twenty five!" he says, eyes lighting up. "She's got an ass that can go for miles, and her tits? Geez, lose my face in them if I could. And boy, when she gets mad—whew!" Frank makes a high whistle, shaking his head. "You've never seen the Fourth of July until you've seen Bethany Pekowski chase down the neighbor's beagle. I mean, damn. Make a man hard just thinking about it."

"Tell her," I demand. "Get your phone out right now, and say that."

"What?" Frank goes pale, his hand dropping to his gun like it can protect him. "I can't just—"

"You can," Roar argues, and motions for Harmony to take over his job of blocking the camera. "And this is how you tell a woman you love her."

Roar steps in front of me and holds out a hand, almost as if he's asking me to dance. Or to trust him. I don't even hesitate. My hand slides into his and he spins me in one smooth motion so that my back is to him. Then he wraps both arms around my waist, and pulls me in close, my butt fitting snugly against him.

"No space between you," Roar explains to Frank. "Start like this, with the cuddle. Firm grip around the middle lets her know it is not nap time." Roar demonstrates, pulling me even tighter against his body. Despite myself I can't stop a little gasp escaping. "You see, she feels my manhood and is impressed by its firmness and length."

I feel like I ought to protest, even though he's totally right—I am impressed by its firmness and length. But Frank's brow is furrowed like he's really trying to take this lesson in, and I don't want to get in the way of his progress.

"You let her relax for a moment," Roar continues. "Then, you move her hair. Does your woman have long hair?"

"Yes," Frank nods, watching Roar closely so as not to miss any hot tips.

"Her hair will likely be wrapped around her neck, fun in some situations but not in the I love you times. Move her hair..."

Roar fingers trail over my neck, gripping the shock of hair that has twisted under my ear lobe.

"Don't pull it, though," I say, trying to keep my tone businesslike, as my heart hammers in my chest.

"Pulling has uses, but not in this moment," Roar agrees, gently tugging my hair away from my neck. It falls down my back and he leans in more closely.

"Do not shave before you go to your woman," Roar instructs, grinding his stubble against the soft skin of my neck. "Let her feel your manliness here, and here." His grip around my hips tightens, and he pushes against me. Without meaning to, I wiggle a little.

"But don't give her stubble burn," I advise, my voice a little more high-pitched than usual. "A woman doesn't want to wake up with a rash."

"Stubble burn is an easy way to mark your woman," Roar argues. "Also, teeth marks."

"Okay, I don't—" I'm about to pull away from him when there's a quick pulse of pressure on my earlobe, a light nip that makes me gasp. The arm around my waist tightens, and my breath becomes shaky.

"Then you lean in," Roar says. "Wait a moment, let her wonder if there is another nibble coming."

I have to admit, I am curious.

But then all of my physical sensations are washed away as Roar whispers roughly in my ear, "I love you."

Black spots roll through my vision, and my stomach drops. I want to spin in his arms, lock his mouth to mine and grind against him until neither of us can stand it anymore, stripping off our clothes and—

"So that works?" Frank asks.

"Huh?" I roll back toward him, mouth slack, eyes unfocused.

"For fuck's sake," Harmony mutters, obviously much less moved by this demonstration.

"Sugar crashing again?" Frank asks, sounding legitimately concerned.

"No, I'm...I have to pee."

It's not *not* true. There's definitely some pressure down there that could be a bladder situation.

"Oh, I can take you," Frank comes to his feet and straightens his gun, all business again. Harmony moves away from the camera as Roar also gets up. I can't look at him, and I don't make eye contact as Frank swipes his ID card against a flat panel next to the door.

"To the right," Frank says, as we move through a purely white hallway, the water on one side sending shimmering patterns across the opposite wall. "Sorry, but I've got to come in with you," he says when I get to a paneled door with the figure of a mermaid etched onto it.

"It's okay," I tell him. I'm pretty sure he was one of the guards in the room when I was strip searched earlier, so it's not like it matters. I attend to business, and after I've washed and dried my hands, Frank asks me to look at a text he's composed for his wife.

Bethany, I love where your tits are when you chase dogs. I want to sleep with you touching and chew on your ear and not snore anymore because I'm empty inside.

"Good?" he asks, eyes full of hope.

"Maybe some tweaks?" I put my hand out and he gives me the phone. I change the message so he sounds less like a serial killer and more like a man desperately trying to get his wife back.

But that's all I do. I don't try to dial 911. I don't try to send an SOS to anyone.

I fix a bad text with good intentions into a loving message with the right tone.

Because karma, dammit.

14

———

I sleep well, and try not to attribute it to the fact that I'm in Roar's arms again. We are all cuddled in a ball, lying on a flat floor in a cold room. And I'm perfectly comfortable. Except he *is* snoring. I consider his claim that he just needs to be emptied, and wonder if Harmony wasn't here what I might do to help alleviate the situation.

I roll away from him, eyeing the fish on the other side of the glass wall. They are gliding peacefully, completely unaware that I am lost, confused, and in great danger. I place my palm against the glass, feel the cold pressure of the water. There's a calmness to it, and I slide into something of a trance, sleep still clinging to the edges of my consciousness.

Hello?

I step back from the glass, confused. I close my eyes, reaching out with my mind.

Hepa?

The visual I had from her yesterday when I asked how to destroy the *talentum* was a pile of salt, streams of white particles flowing down all the sides. I know enough about the magical properties of salt to understand that she's asking if it will block the *talentum*'s capabilities, but I also don't know where a person is supposed to get that much salt.

But I'm not getting anything from Hepa this morning. Whatever communication I'd been able to establish with her is no longer functioning. I sigh, and rest my head against the glass. I'm immediately rushed with visuals, particles flowing, movement, a great desire, and an intense pressure. It's like when Roar whispered into my ear during our role play with Frank.

I jerk back from the glass, and am rubbing the spot on my forehead when the door slides open. Busk walks in, trailed by Frank, who looks decidedly...emptied. And very pleased with himself.

"Good morning," Busk says, rubbing his hands together. "I apologize for the delay in our affairs. Some things had to be put in order for the next stage of our relationship to progress. I trust everyone slept well?"

Harmony gives him a dirty look while adjusting a kink in her neck, while Roar just growls.

"I slept fine, thanks," I inform him, stepping forward. "I'd like to go home now, and I'm taking my mother with me. You will also restore Roar's berserker abilities before we leave."

Busk considers me for a second, then throws his head back and laughs. So much for the power of positive thinking.

"You're adorable," he says. "As I said yesterday, I won't be releasing any of you any time soon. You owe me a *talentum*, and your mother's capabilities would work well within my network. Also, you've caught my attention in other ways, dear Crystal. My employee here was late to work this morning for the first time in years."

Frank blushes, looking down at the floor. "Sorry about that, boss."

"Don't be sorry!" Busy says, opening his arms wide. "I can't tell you how glad I was to hear about your...reunion with Bethany. It's so good to know that just one session with Crystal could have such an instant effect."

"You told him?" I ask, my voice rising in accusation.

"He didn't necessarily tell me," Busk says, with a smile. "He was so overjoyed with his, ahem, victories on the home front that he was sharing the news of his marital bliss with a coworker. I just happened to overhear." Busk spins his finger in the air, no doubt indicating the ever-present listening devices, and the tabs he likely keeps on his employees, as well as prisoners. "I was so glad to hear about the positive effects you had on my loyal employee and his wife."

"Fantastic effect," Frank pipes up, the rifle dropping slightly. Roar sidles to the left as the muzzle temporarily aligns with his crotch. "I figured we were doomed to a life of living like roommates. One session with Crystal and BANG!"

"And he does mean BANG. You know the oldest saying in the ad industry, right?" Busk asks, a glimmer of darkness passing over his eyes. "Sex sells."

"I don't peddle in that," I bite back, pointing an accusatory finger at Busk. "It's love that I can help mend. Physical connection is only a small part of that."

"Not for most of us, dearest," Busk says. "And if you've got the goods—the real goods—I'm sitting on a goldmine. I'm thinking of a dating app." He spreads his hands, eyes unfocused as he envisions his next money maker. "Sex Signs."

"I've seen those on the highway," Roar mutters.

"That's not what he means," I shout, pointing at Busk. "He wants to use my talents of mending relationships as a way to make a quick buck with cheap hookups."

"And if it mends a few marriages along the way, that's great publicity," Busk says. "So settle in, ladies. Nobody is going anywhere. I've got my next business to launch, and if I can use one of you to grant curses and the other for some sexual healing, that would be great. You're assets now, so sit tight. But first, I'm going to become a god."

"Or just a bigger asshole," I say under my breath.

"Or that," he agrees with a shrug. "But in the meantime, I need that *talentum*. You know I'm not going to trade your mother for it, so any goodwill or trust we had established has gone out the window. I'll ask once, nicely, and then things may have to get a little more...forceful."

I gulp, my pulse racing.

"Crystal," he says calmly, gaze leveling with mine. "Where is your piece of the *talentum*?"

I have to buy time. Maddie may not have had the chance to plant the fake *talentum* at the wharf yet. I can't risk Busk sending his goons to find out it's not there. Or worse—catch Maddie planting the fake. I straighten my shoulders and stick my chin out.

"I'll never tell."

Frank groans and shakes his head. "Not the wise choice, Crystal."

"No, it isn't," Busk muses. "And unfortunately, my associate's dick isn't going to be the only thing that's wet around here."

"Ew," I say. "What a crass way to talk about the miracle of lovemaking."

"Perhaps this man has never made love," Roar says.

Busk laughs again. "Do you think I'm a virgin? I'm a billionaire. I could have a horde of prostitutes here in minutes if I wanted."

"Having sex..." I start to say.

"Isn't making love," Roar finishes.

"How quaint you are," Busk tells us as he leads us down the hallway, me trailing with Harmony and Roar behind us. Frank brings up the rear, all business now that things are going the wrong direction for us. He makes it clear where his loyalties lie.

Busk leads us into a circular room made of glass. The sea surrounds us on all sides; even the floor is glass. It's beautiful...except for the torture device in the middle.

"No, you can't!" Harmony cries out, grabbing my hand.

"I thought this might be upsetting for you," Busk agrees, nodding. "It's a reproduction of a witch-dunking tank.

Unfortunately, I wasn't able to acquire a usable antique. However, there was a fellow on Etsy who was happy to make some discreet income."

I swallow, my throat closing up as I look at the wooden pool with a seesaw attached to the side. It would look like a child's toy...if it wasn't for the manacles.

"I wondered what would be best. Drown mom? Or drown daughter? Who is likely to break first?" Busk asks, tapping his chin as if in deep thought. "And then I realized—I don't care!"

Casually, he pulls a coin from his pocket and turns to Roar. "Heads or tails?"

"I will not play your games, money man," Roar says.

"But games are so much fun," he protests, slipping the coin back into his pocket. "Alright, fine. I'll pick." He considers the two of us, and Harmony's hand twitches in mine. I remember her refusing to take me to the beach as a child, her fear of the water and inability to swim overriding any parental urges to allow her child to fit in socially.

"Take me," I say, stepping forward.

"No." Roar pulls me back and tugs me behind him, as if Busk removing me from the guy's sight will make him lose interest.

I give Roar's bicep a pat for him and then a squeeze for me. He's so firm and manly, it would be easy to hide in his shadow and let him fight my battles for me. Unfortunately, that would just end with a bunch of goons beating Roar until he looks like ground beef. And that would be more painful than anything Busk has planned for me.

"Roar," I say to him. "I know you came here to protect me... but the reason I let you come was because I needed emotional support."

Roar frowns. "But you wear a bra for that."

"Oh for fuck's sake," Harmony mutters and then louder adds, "Crystal needs you to tell her she is wise and wonderful and strong. That's it. She's already got me to tell her she's an idiot for coming here, and volunteering for torture makes her an even bigger one."

"I see," Roar says. "You need someone to believe in you."

"I believe in her," Harmony nearly snarls in a way that makes me think he hit a nerve. "I just don't agree with her stupid choices."

Roar nods slowly and I can almost see him thinking. "Being tortured is a stupid choice," he says, but then adds, "But you are younger than your mother, even if you are past your prime birthing years."

"Okay, I don't think we need to bring age into this," I say. And then quickly add, "Which is just a number."

"Can we move this along?" Busk snipes.

"I support you," Roar says, clapping a hand on each of my shoulders. "Remember, the torture will be terrible, but the nightmares afterwards will be even worse."

"Oh boy," Harmony mutters. "I think you should've stuck with your bra for support."

I decide to ignore her even though I suspect she may be right. "Thank you, Roar," I say. Then I turn to Busk. "We're all set here. I'll go first."

"You'll go *first*," Busk corrects. "But remember, if you break, that means Harmony won't have to go at all."

It's cruel and vindictive—and I'm sure incredibly effective. But I have no intention of letting Harmony go. If I drag this out, I'll "confess" before she can get tortured.

"Are you sure?" Frank asks me. "Just tell him what he wants to know. He always gets his way. There's no point in torturing yourself."

"Frank!" Busk glares at him. "I did not hire you to help me negotiate."

"Yes sir!" Frank says, snapping to attention and shutting his mouth tight.

Busk turns to me. "But he's not wrong. Last chance. If you tell me everything now, we can part as friends. We won't wet a hair on your head."

I turn to him. "You and I are *not* friends."

I make my way to the device. Frank stands on the end of the plank to keep it from dipping under my weight as I climb to the end. I look at him. "I don't blame you for this," I tell Frank. He nods, shamefaced.

Busk comes to the edge of the pool, fastening the manacles to my wrists and ankles. I look up at the ceiling, where light from the water below me plays across the blank white space in intricate and beautiful patterns. I close my eyes, panic slipping in. God, I don't know how long I can last. Hopefully long enough for Maddie to plant the fake *talentum*.

"All right," Busk says calmly, stepping away from the side of the pool. "Dunk her."

It happens fast, the water rushing over my face before I have time to take a deep breath. My hair fans out around me, and I struggle against the restraints, even though I know it's pointless. My body wants to live, even though my mind knows I can't break the manacles. I hear shouting and screaming, but it's muted by the water and the sound of my own thrashing.

Me fighting against the restraints has made me burn up what little oxygen I had. I toss my head, resisting the burning urge to open my mouth, to breathe in.

Hello?

There is again, the voice from this morning. It's small and quiet. Curious. I stop fighting, my hair floating around me like a wreath. Images fill my head, water molecules and rushing fluid, the red pulse of my lungs and the cold water wanting to push inside.

No, wait, I think.

Suddenly, I'm jerked upwards, leaving the water like a punch to the gut. I take a deep breath of air, tossing my head to throw my soaked hair off my face.

"You son of a bitch, you fucking coward, you..."

I don't know who is talking, whether it's Roar or Harmony, which seems like it should be an easy distinction to make. Then I hear Frank's voice, a quiet undertone.

"Now!" he says, and I take his advice, gulping in a huge breath of air before he drops me again. This time, when the water rushes into my ears, I'm ready.

It's just like with the dew the other day. I can feel each drop, know its origin story. Some of it is rain, some has come from the Gulf of Mexico, some was poured in from a Dasani bottle. Each molecule competes for attention, wanting something from me, needing me...wanting me.

Once again, I get the image of my lungs, red and full, bursting. The water presses, showing me what it would look like if I allowed it in, air sacs filing with water. There's a brief shudder of music, a calming surge that almost makes me compliant. I'd always been told that drowning people hear music, but I never realized it was because the water was romancing them, showing them the easy way out.

NO, I tell it. I send a different visual, my lungs breathing, functioning, pulling in oxygen, while the water waits, resting outside of my body, rolling over my skin, filling my eyes and ears and...well, everything. But not going into my nose or mouth or lungs.

The water pauses, considering. It's...interested.

I think of Maddie and Helena, how they command wind and earth, bending it to their will, forcing their powers onto nature. That's not my way, and I won't force my will upon anything.

Listen, please, I think instead, showing the water my acceptance and love, just as red begins to fill my vision. I'm going to have to surface soon, or die. I can hear screaming, but I'm not fighting anymore, just pushing all my thoughts toward the water, asking it to understand me.

Suddenly, it pushes back, showing me something new.

It's a water molecule, H2O, and a picture of my lungs filling with it. But it's not a threat—because water has oxygen in it as well.

Try the water asks.

And I open my mouth, and pull water into my lungs.

15

I can breathe underwater.

Okay, it's not breathing, not taking in oxygen and pushing out carbon dioxide. The water sits in my lungs and my body—somehow—takes what it needs from the liquid, the water allowing the oxygen molecules to feed my lungs. It's like it's making a choice. The choice to not kill me.

I let out a laugh and no bubbles glug to the surface. There's just a stream of water coming from my mouth, like I'm singing liquid. It's amazing, empowering, fantastic. I could stay down here forever.

Except I can't. There's pressure against my face as water rushes past my cheeks, Frank raising the other side of the dunking machine and pulling me up into the air. My face breaks the water and I expel the water from my lungs with a cough.

"You're drowning her," Roar shouts. He rushes toward me but another guard swings to train a gun on him, and the

Viking pulls up short, chest heaving. With his berserker powers gone, he's just a regular human trying to save me.

But he doesn't know I don't need saving.

"Are you ready to talk?" Busk asks me.

I shake my head, spit more water into his direction. I catch Harmony's eyes and she sees the fire in mine.

Crystal...?

I'm fine. I send to her mentally. *This is going to sound insane but—"* Busk dunks me again and when I'm submerged I don't even hesitate. *I can breathe underwater.*

Harmony sends a mental cackle of glee. *Your powers are coming in! This is amazing! And you can breathe underwater? That's way better than what Maddie and Helena got. Fate saved the best for last!*

I want to agree but I'm jerked upward again and the first thing I see again is Roar. Harmony knows that I'm okay, but there's no way to assure him that I'm not going to die right in front of him without tipping off Busk as well.

"She's not breathing," Roar screams and I realize I'd forgotten to release the water from my lungs. To him, I probably look like I'm dead. Which...could be to my advantage. If I pretend to pass out, Busk can't question me. Maybe he'll lose his stomach for torture. Or maybe he'll just strap Harmony in next.

That's too horrible of a thought; and Harmony can't breathe underwater. I cough and choke, sputtering. "I'm not drowned," I tell them. "I just need...a moment..."

"Again!" Busk shouts.

Before he submerges me I wink at Roar. Hopefully, he'll see I'm not under real duress. Hopefully he doesn't pop a blood vessel trying to fight to get to me. When I break the surface again, Roar has gone slack, his muscles useless, his temper gone. He looks like a man beaten by his captors. But he returns the wink, and I fight the urge to sing, "I know something you don't know," at Busk before I get dunked again.

It's a good thirty minutes before Busk grows bored, stretching out the length of keeping me underwater to a full minute, and then ninety seconds. But I won't break, and each session without air brings me into closer commune with the water.

"Enough!" Busk declares and orders Frank to untie me. He helps me off the board and I fall to the glass floor. Wet and shivering, I glare at Busk.

"Time to punish the old woman," he says.

"No!" I hold up my hand. I hope that Maddie has had enough time, that I bought enough room for her to duplicate the *talentum* and place the fake at the warehouse where we all met. "I'll tell you..." I pretend to choke. Every second could count.

"I'm getting impatient," Busk says as he puts a grasping hand on Harmony's shoulder. Her eyes go wide with a real terror that she can't hide. I might be able to breathe underwater, but she sure as hell can't.

I can't delay any longer. "The piece, it's at the wharf where this all started. Where Bobby tried to become a god, but it backfired," I say. "He ended up dead and you will too, because you're not worthy."

I glance up from where I'm dripping, my hair in wet sheets on either side of my face. I know it's a stab in the dark, but maybe he can be convinced that the *talentum* will be the death of him. After seeing Bobby erupt into a pillar of fire, I can't imagine anyone would want to take that chance.

"Don't be stupid," Busk sneers. "I've spent a lot of time considering this 'worthiness' issue." He puts air quotes around worthiness, like having moral fiber is something that can be established by what he eats every morning. "The power is there to be taken, and it clearly wants to distribute itself just about anywhere. If a housewife and stay-at-home mom can be elevated to goddess status, imagine what the *talentum* will do for me?"

"Gross," I spit. Being a mediocre white male really is empowering.

"And besides," he continues, "I also plan to have an entire cadre of witches and warlocks at my side when I assemble the *talentum*. For every action there is an equal and opposite reaction, and the magical world is not so different from ours. My employees will make sure that any negative intent the *talentum* has will be funneled elsewhere. Whereas I will come into my powers right away."

"And you still won't be happy," Harmony tells him.

"I'll have everything I want." Busk grins.

"Not the same thing," she says, shaking her head.

"I don't give a shit if you're happy or not," I say, spitting out the last vestiges of water from my lungs. "I gave you what you wanted. Now let us go!" I shout.

"You know I won't," Busk says smugly. "I mean, really, what world do you people live in?"

Roar pushes through his guards, but Busk nods for them to allow it. He lifts me to my feet and holds me close to his chest.

"I'm fine," I tell him. He looks me over, concern clouding his blue eyes. I lean into him, as if needing his strength for support. Instead, my lips find his ear. "I'll explain later, but I promise, that wasn't torturous for me."

"What a touching scene," Busk coos in a syrupy voice. "Enjoy your man while you can, Crystal, because I recently received some bad news from R&D."

A lump forms in my throat as I recall that Busk told us that the thing he shot came from research and development—and it was still experimental.

Roar clearly recalls it too, because he straightens and looks Busk clear in the eye. "What is going to happen to me?"

Busk laughs aloud. "Nothing good, I'm afraid. Or perhaps I should say, *she'll* be afraid. Of you." He points to me.

"Never." Lifting my chin, I wrap both hands around one of Roar's giant biceps. "I could never be afraid of him."

"I hoped you would say that." Busk gives another evil chuckle. It's like he spent a semester at villain school mastering the varieties of nasty laughs. "Because it turns out that the little blast he received turning off his powers was not permanent after all. And apparently when his powers come back there's a bit of a rebound effect, as all that magic that's been jammed up inside of him builds up quite a bit of pressure, when it releases."

"Boom," Harmony says in a low voice.

Busk grins. "Exactly."

Roar removes my hand from his arm and steps back from me. "You must lock me away from all others. Immediately."

"No!" I protest at the same time that Busk shakes his head.

"No can do. Or no *will* do, to be more accurate. The lady here said very clearly that she isn't afraid of you."

"She is an emotional, foolish woman," Roar says. "You cannot listen to her."

"I do agree with you on the first part of that statement," Busk says. "But as to the second, I think I'd rather indulge her. How else will she learn?"

"No!" Harmony steps between Busk and Roar. "I'll kill him if you put him in the same room with me and Crystal."

"Harmony!" I cry out while Busk's smile just gets larger.

"Oh, this is an interesting little triangle. I may have security save the film from this to watch back later, like my own personal soap opera." Busk glances at his watch, something large and ostentatious. "But I'm afraid this episode is at its end. I need to prepare for the ceremony tonight."

"You son of a bitch," Harmony spits and then before she can say another word, a guard stuffs a rag into her mouth and carries her away.

Busk shakes his head fondly. "Her curses are charming, but I just don't have time to deal with that right now. Hopefully she'll cool off, because I'd planned on bringing her along to see the ceremony. You too, Crystal." He flicks a finger in my direction. And then adds, "If you're still alive." With that parting line, Busk exits and the guards take hold of me and Roar.

"No! Lock me up alone!" Roar yells, and despite not having his berserker abilities, it takes four guards to restrain him.

I go without a struggle while Roar is dragged behind me, thrashing and kicking the whole way. But it makes no difference. The door to a new prison cell is opened and the two of us are pushed inside. The door closes with a heavy thud.

16

This room is different than the plain cell we'd been occupying. It's more like a cheap honeymoon motel room with a big heart-shaped bed and an en suite bathroom. The effect, though, is ruined by the walls which look to be made of solid reinforced steel, thick enough to keep a raging rhino—or furious berserker—from breaking out.

Roar collapses to his knees, cradling his head in his hands. "Go into the bathroom," he tells me. "Lock the door. I will barricade myself in on this side."

I kneel next to him and gently place my hands on his head. "Busk could be wrong about what's going to happen. Or he could be lying. Let's not panic."

He looks up at me, his expression stark. "I cannot kill the woman I love. Not again."

This knocks me back. Literally. I tumble onto my butt.

As I stare at Roar, my brain takes that sentence and breaks it apart.

I focus on the "woman I love" bit first as it's the nice part. More than nice. It's...revelatory. Roar loves me. He loves me. I mean, sure, as far as declarations of love go, this one was a little lacking in flowers and butterflies. Then again...Bobby gave me all the flowers and butterflies—along with a big heap of bullshit.

Roar, though, tells it like it is—or at least how he thinks it is. I'd like to believe that he's wrong about this whole killing the woman he loves—again—bit. Because that means he loved someone else and it maybe worked out even worse than things did for me and Bobby.

I get to my feet, realizing that all the questions filling my head can only be answered by Roar. But I'd rather not let all of Busk's goons listen in.

"I need to get cleaned up, and so do you," I tell Roar, and then tug at his hands until he reluctantly gets to his feet and follows.

Once in the bathroom, I turn on the shower at full blast, hot water immediately pooling out in curtains and misting up the bathroom.

Roar stands in the door, uncertain. I pull him in, put my mouth close to his ear. I hope that the steam and the noise of the shower will just make this look and sound like a lover's embrace, for the benefit of any cameras in the room.

"Get in the shower," I tell him. "I have the power to control water, if you attack, I'll drown you. Okay?"

For the first time since Busk's surprise revelation, Roar actually looks hopeful. "I would happily let you murder me," he says.

I wince at his wording and have to bite my tongue to keep from telling him that I would never ever kill him, no matter what was happening. For now, though, it's better to let him think that I will defend myself.

Fully clothes, I step into the shower beside Roar, and then take a moment to close my eyes and have a little chat with the water molecules all around me.

Hey guys, there's lots of cameras and microphones in here. Can you fog up the cameras and fill the mics with sounds of rushing water? Don't disable them, just hide me and Roar.

The water's only reply is a gurgle that to me sounds like a yes. I smile and hold out a hand, watching the beads of water roll down my arm and settle into my palm.

Thank you, I say to it.

"We can talk privately," I tell Roar. "The water is hiding us."

He nods at this. "You have your powers now, then?"

I smile, feeling a little bashful about it. The word *powers* feels wrong for what's happening. It's more like...I've made a new friend. "I can commune with water," I tell him. "Which I sort of guessed would happen, since Maddie has air and Helena is earth. But..." I hesitate, as I try to recall if anything else has manifested. "I still am not sure what my crab powers are." I do a slow circle, holding out my arms so Roar can see my whole body. "There aren't any weird crab parts coming out of me, are there?"

"No. Just woman. Beautiful woman." Roar gazes at me with obvious appreciation.

My eyes fill with tears of happiness and also regret, because the timing on this sucks. Still, there's nothing to be done for it. I can sit and cry or I can seize the day. And I intend to seize.

"Roar, do you love me? Is that what you said before?"

His shoulders sag in defeat. "I have tried not to. But from the first moment I set eyes on you—everything in you called to me."

I gasp aloud as my heart painfully expands. "I felt the same way. But I didn't quite trust it. I thought it was just animal magnetism."

"Yes," Roar agrees. "At first I felt it in my loins. But the more time we spent together, the more the feeling has moved here." Roar places a hand over his heart. "And here." His other hand covers the top of his head. "That is when I knew I loved you and that I must get as far away as possible to save you from myself."

I'd been ready to throw my arms around him, until the end of this speech when it takes a sharp turn and veers off a cliff. "That is the dumbest thing I ever heard!" I tell him. "Well, not the first part, but you don't run away from someone you love!"

"To keep you safe! I had to!" Roar protests. "Except you were already in danger, so I had to stay...until you were safe. Then I could leave."

I eye him skeptically. "Sounds like a pickle."

"Yes, it was sour," Roar agrees.

"Oh, Roar." My annoyance flees. How can I stay mad at this dumb lug? "I love you too, and I am not letting you run away."

"I would have ridden Velvet Thunder. He is very fast."

I shake my head. "It doesn't matter. I would've found you." I reach for his hands. "I love you too. Don't you get it?"

"You do?" He looks at me with wonder on his face. But that quickly turns to despair. "You must not. It is no good."

"Yeah, I understand you feel that way. Maybe, though, we can delve a bit more into the why?" I sit on the floor of the shower, cross-legged, and pull Roar down beside me. "Tell me about your past. Who died?"

"My wife," Roar says.

"Your wife?" I gasp, strangely hurt. "You never mentioned her before. Even when I told you about Bobby."

Roar shrugs. "It was hundreds of years ago."

"Still," I protest.

"And it is a painful memory," he adds, looking confused by why I'm upset. "I do not speak of Gertrud ever. Not since her death."

"But you're speaking of her now," I prompt.

"Yes," Roar agrees. "It is time. Once you hear, you will understand why you must get away from me and give me your love no more."

"Yeah, that's not how love works," I tell him. "But let's not argue about that. Tell me."

Wanting to make it easier for him, I turn around so that my back is to him. It's sometimes easier to say painful things when you don't have to look at the other person's face. But I still want us to be connected, so I scooch backwards until I'm in his lap. After a moment of hesitation, his arms close around me.

"This is not wise," he rumbles, but his arms remain around me.

"We'll be wise later," I reassure him, although honestly if wise means being far away from each other, then I'd rather be foolish.

"I was a warrior, a Viking," Roar starts, his voice low in my ear. "But our village was small and we feared for the safety of our families. We heard that a neighboring village had received help from a man who granted powers to the best of their warriors, making them undefeatable. But when we went to seek out this village, it was gone." Roar sighs heavily and I can feel it where our bodies connect.

"We should have taken that clue and left it. Instead, we hunted this man, believing more than ever that he was the only answer. We found him almost too easily...another hint we failed to perceive. It was also not difficult to persuade him to give us the same powers."

"How?" I ask, my voice soft.

"This man was a hunter of monsters. Monsters we had always believed were best left alone. But he told us there was no other way. He had us hunt a wyvern. Do you know of such creatures?"

I shake my head.

"Not many do," Roar answers. "Once they were not uncommon, then rare, and finally they disappeared altogether. They were small dragon-like creatures and they breathed fire."

"Oh," I say. "They must have been beautiful."

"No," Roar says. "They were hideous scaled beasts, but they were…majestic. To see them fly over the sea, bursts of fire escaping their mouths, it took my breath away."

"But you killed one."

"We did. Each of us who had agreed to become one of the super warriors." Roar tucks me in closer to him, almost as if he needs the comfort. "My wife, my Gertrud, did not want me to do it. She warned that it was unnatural. In some ways, she reminds me of you. She was gentle, much like you. Even wringing a chicken's neck was done with a sweetness."

I can't help a little shudder from going through me at the thought of having to wring a chicken's neck. But maybe if I'd been raised as a Viking woman instead of a vegan, I'd do it without a second thought.

"I should have listened to Gertrud," Roar continues, "but I did not. Instead, I killed the wyvern and ate its heart while it was still warm and bloody."

"Oh!" I gasp, the word forced out of me at the horribleness of this.

Roar's arms release me. "You wish to go now? You see already what I am?"

I grab hold of each of his wrists and pull his arms so that they are around me once more. "You just surprised me is all. Maybe a 'horrible things are coming' warning next time you're going to tell a story that includes eating a still-beating heart, okay?"

Roar gives a hollow little laugh. "Consider this your warning, then; horrible things are coming. The wyvern was the least of it. Though we did not know it at the time. We suffered a long night on the high cliffs over the sea where the wyvern were found. We sweated and shivered and panted with thirst that no water could quench. One man, unable to take it any longer, tossed himself into the sea. The rest of us were not as wise. We survived to see the morning. We let the wyvern's heart of fire burn through us."

"We were no longer men; we were monsters ourselves."

17

———

I gulp. Roar is not usually poetic in his speech, but I have a feeling this is a story he has told himself many times over the years.

I snuggle into Roar's chest, while gently rubbing the place over his heart; I can actually feel the pain emanating from it. How can I feel that? I don't know. But I do.

"The man who led us to these powers told us then that our rages would be uncontrollable. That when ordered to attack we'd fight until there was no blood left to spill. We did not quite believe him. And then he told us that he himself was our new commander. We laughed."

"He didn't take that well?" I ask.

"We did not expect him to," Roar says. "He was a small sickly-looking man with a limp. We thought him weak for not taking a wyvern of his own. But we were the weak ones. He proved that easily enough. We went back to our village and he followed. Meekly. We thought we'd put him in his place. He was merely waiting. Our families ran out to greet us. My Gertrud, I can still see the relief on her face that I had returned in one piece, no worse for wear. Or so we thought."

Roar stops abruptly and the pain coming from him is so raw that I throw myself against him and press both my hands against his heart as if I can stop it from breaking. But of course it already broke all those years ago. Shattered into a million fragments. And despite all the time that has passed, remembering makes the pain come back almost like it is fresh again.

"I—" Roar starts, but I press my lips against his, stopping his words. I don't need to hear the rest, I can see it, feel it, telling me what happened with every beat of his heart.

The man—who sounds like some sort of evil wizard to me —ordered the Vikings to attack their own village. And they did. Their eyes went white, a killing rage took over them, and they were totally unprepared for it. They killed their wives and children, their fathers and mothers, sisters and brothers. They killed everyone until only the berserkers were left.

After that the evil wizard led them and other berserkers in various raids for some time—it's not clear from Roar's memories. Eventually the bad wizard guy messed with a witch and she ripped him a new one. I never before knew that wasn't just a euphemism, but if Roar's memories are accurate, that's exactly what happened. Some of the berserkers went on killing and stuff, but Roar went off on his own. He became a recluse, at first hopeless and then slowly attempting to master his own powers with meditation. Throughout all those years he never again loved or laid with a woman—

Pulling away from Roar, I snap upright. "Whoa! You haven't done it since you did it with your wife?"

Roar's cheeks turn faintly pink. "You have heard me snore."

"But what about all that stuff about women wanting your seed?"

He shrugs. "Women do want my seed. But I cannot risk giving it to them."

I still can't believe it. "But..." I sputter. "How..."

Roar holds out his hands in a 'I don't know' type gesture. "Has it been hard?" He nods, answering his own question. "Often. This is why I take cold showers." Blushing even redder he adds in a low voice, "I also sometimes take matters into my own hands."

"Oh, Roar." I reach for him, my heart overflowing with love and compassion for this beautiful man. "You're practically a virgin."

At this, he frowns. "I pleased Gertrud many times. She screamed with pleasure."

Jealousy surges up in me and I say for both my and Roar's benefit, "A heck of a long time ago." And then because I can imagine he might feel jealous of my past lovers too, I add, "It's been a long time for me too."

This isn't a lie exactly. I haven't been with anyone since Bobby and that was a year ago, but so much has happened since then that it feels even longer. Especially when I've got Maddie and Helena finding true love and amazing sexy times right beneath my nose.

Also, one year of my short life is probably percentage-wise around the same as hundreds of Roar's many years. I mean, let's not actually do the math on that, but just say that theoretically it works out.

"You can barely remember the pleasure of a man's body?" Roar asks.

"Almost not at all," I answer. I pull my soaking wet shirt off over my head, letting my bra roll off with it. "We can both be brand new again. Together."

Roar looks at my chest like a man who has not let himself look at a naked woman's chest in a long time. "I wished that Busk's gun would work forever, that the wyvern had left my body. That I could let myself love you."

I shake my head at him. "But you were so upset about losing your powers!"

"Because I wanted to protect you! Because it is all I have known for a very long time. But a small part of me hoped to dream…"

He looks at me with equal parts longing and hopelessness.

"Listen, bub," I say, taking his hands in mine. "You are not the guy you were that night Gertrud died. You told me when you fought Helena that first time that you were not fully in the berserker rage. So you must have some control."

"Some, yes," he admits. "And yet I nearly killed her."

"But Ford stopped you," I remind him. "And then you snapped out of it."

"Yes, I did but…" Roar agrees, his gaze drifting from my eyes down to my chest. Normally, I'd disapprove of that type of thing, but in this case, I'll allow it. In fact, I'll even help him along. I take his hands and place them against my breasts. Roar goes tense for a minute and I wonder if he's gonna lose his seed right there and then, but he controls himself. A sort of dreamy look enters his face as his hands mold themselves to me.

"Can you feel my heart?" I ask him.

"No, just boobs," he answers, his voice full of incredulous joy.

I laugh despite myself. "Well, I heard your heart, and not just the beating. It's like what was inside of you spoke to me. I think..." I hesitate as I work through the thought just occurring to me. "I think it's my power. My crab power."

Roar pauses in caressing my breasts to look at me. "Crabs talk to hearts?"

"Well, no, I don't think so, "I admit. "But I've been researching them quite a bit out of curiosity. They can regrow limbs, which is cool, and I thought that might be my power, although it doesn't seem very useful, I mean, how often does one lose a limb?"

"It happens," Roar says, but he's only half paying attention again as he tweaks one of my nipples.

"Ooh!" I say and that's enough to get me off track for a few minutes before I swat Roar's hand away. "Don't distract me," I say, my voice husky. "I'm trying to tell you about crabs."

"Right." Roar removes his hands from my chest. "I cannot have you anyway and it is wrong too—"

I give him a shove. "Stop that! I'm gonna have you ten ways to Tuesday, but just let me finish our talk first, okay?"

Roar frowns. "We shouldn't..."

It's a perfunctory protest and we both know it. Roar's balls are so blue he doesn't have the will to resist me, even if he's afraid of what happens when his berserker side comes back.

"Crabs have eyes that can see a lot and they have antennas for sensing stuff. I think my powers are the ability to see into other people—like their true essence. I felt it the other day when we were working with Frank too. Like I could feel the good in him."

Roar takes this in and then points to his chest. "If you can feel the good, then you can also feel the bad. Find the wyvern, hear its hunger for blood. Then if you still want me..." He pauses, gulps, and then closes his eyes as if fighting against some sort of exquisite brand of pain. "Then I will bed you."

"Nope, no beds," I say. "Too many cameras in there. But we can do it all over this bathroom."

"I would like this," Roar agrees, his voice hoarse. "But first —" He picks up my hands and presses them to his chest. "Find the beast."

A part of me wants to pretend to do it and then tell Roar I didn't find anything. But that wouldn't be fair to him. And it would be cowardly. Taking a deep breath, I close my eyes and let myself feel Roar once again—from the inside out. There is his big heart, thumping wildly; it is scarred from his past trauma, but despite that, hopeful for the future. I love that heart—it is everything that is Roar.

And yet...beneath or behind or maybe even hidden inside it, there is a darkness. A shadow. I want to flinch away, but instead push forward, focusing all my energy toward it. The darkness grows; it's an energy, a wildness—but not made of anger or spite as I feared. It is simply what is left of the wyvern's spirit. It has melded with Roar, changing him, but is also—I believe—being changed as well.

Now I understand why Busk's spell couldn't have worked forever. This is a part of Roar; it can't be cut out and it cannot be contained—doing so would eventually kill him, like cutting off the blood flow to a vital limb.

The wyvern will break free and it will be destructive. Like Busk said, it's pent-up pressure releasing. But I think Roar can control it this time. In fact, I think without even knowing it, he's been controlling it for a long time.

But I know he won't believe this. And I won't waste my breath trying to convince him. Not when I have much better plans for us.

L eaving the shower running, I step out and grab a towel. I'm happy to see that in this at least Busk was generous—they are thick and fluffy and there's a whole pile of them. As Roar pokes his head out of the shower to watch me (and my boobs), I make us a bed on the tile floor.

Once it's ready, I hold a hand out to Roar. "Well? What are you waiting for?"

As a man who strips down before he fights, Roar is good at getting naked fast, but his speed this time is way beyond anything I've seen. He rips his shirt and pants off as if they were made of paper. Then he hauls me to him and removes my pants in the same way.

T"No more clothes," he orders.

"No more," I agree.

We sink down onto the towels clinging to one another, our bodies wet and slick and hot.

"Crystal," Roar pants. "I will be gentle."

"The hell you will," I say and then I push him down onto his back and before he can protest again, impale myself on his hard thick length.

"GUH!" Roar says, which is about the level of coherence I expected from a man who hasn't been inside a woman in ages. Luckily, the control he lacks over his vocal cords, isn't mirrored by the part of him that's inside me. Not that I'd blame him for a little early ejaculation—not this time at least.

But he remains rigid as steel inside of me, even as I begin to move, riding him up and down so I can feel the entirety of him. His eyes roll back in his head and more noises of the guh variety come out of him, but at the same time his hips start to move, matching my rhythm.

"Oooh," I say, moving into the incoherent part of our love-making myself.

"Not yet," Roar grunts. And with one smooth move, he flips us so that he is on top. "Man must be on top to give seed," he tells me.

"Oh no, honey, that's not the case." I am patting his chest and about to explain to him that some of the things about sex might've changed since the last time he had it, but I'm distracted when Roar slides his hands beneath me and then shifts my body so that he's hitting the sweet sensitive little flower bud of nerves that makes up my clitoris.

"Roar!" I gasp, my fingers curling into his shoulders, digging in so that I have an anchor when the whole world explodes.

"Crystal!" he, well, roars. And that's it, I tip over into pure feeling; it bursts through me in waves like a tsunami washing away everything I ever thought I knew about sex. With a warrior yell, Roar comes with me, shuddering for several long moments, before collapsing on top of me.

After that, we do it three more times. I keep waiting for Roar to run out of giddy up, but he seems to have a never-ending supply. Finally, we are both content to cuddle and sleep for a bit. I struggle to stay awake, because I want Roar to fall asleep first. I don't have to wait long for him to drift off. His breathing is low and even and just as I suspected...quiet.

Roar was right. No more snoring.

18

———

In the morning, Roar and I indulge in morning sex that lasts into the afternoon. I don't know why Busk hasn't come to get us yet; maybe he's still hoping Roar will go berserker and smash me to bits. I can't bring myself to care about that right now. Not when we're enjoying ourselves so much.

Roar, though, becomes more tense as the hours pass. I know he fears changing, and will be scared no matter how often I reassure him that we can handle it together—as a team.

I convince him to get into the tub, that it will help him relax. Really, though, I'm the one who wants to soak. I've always loved water, as much as Harmony hated it. No, not hated, feared. She told me once that water would take me away from her.

The bathroom is surprisingly nice; I don't even mind that Roar and I don't have use of an actual bed. The tub has a saltwater tap, which probably isn't a huge indulgence considering we're located underneath the ocean.

Roar pads up behind me then slips into the tub, sinking down into the hot water with me on his lap. It's impossible to miss his huge erection. Turning to face him, I wrap my hands around it. "Is this how you pleasured yourself?" I ask him.

He struggles to breathe. "My hands are much larger."

"And softer?" I ask, stroking him.

"Yes," he says and then shakes his head, sending drops of water flying. "No, your hands are soft. I have a man's strong, rough hands."

"I can be strong," I tell him and squeeze him a little tighter, just enough to force a moan out of him. "And rough too," I add, then I lean forward and nip at his pec.

Suddenly Roar stands and I sprawl backwards into the tub. "No. Crystal, no rough play. Do not tempt the beast to come out."

Immediately, I feel guilty. I hadn't even considered that our play could cause that. But of course it would occur to Roar. "Sorry," I say, "I was just having fun."

Roar gulps. "It was fun. I have never had such...fun."

"Please let's have more?" I say, my eyes on his huge cock which has been at full attention this entire time.

Reaching into the soapy water, Roar pulls me up so that I'm facing him. But I have other ideas. I turn and then bend at the waist and grip the edge of the tub.

"You ever do it this way before?" I ask him.

"Of course," Roar answers. "Vikings invented horsie style!"

And then he proceeds to show me exactly how Vikings do it.

Afterwards, we're lounging in the tub, filled with saltwater, when a thought comes to me. "Roar, what do you know about salt?"

"Salt?"

"I know that it can cleanse auras and in a ring can help keep you safe from supernatural attacks. Anything else...maybe something you've learned in your long life?"

He tilts his head. "Salt is a powerful magical deterrent."

I nod. Hepa was cut off before she could say more. And I have no idea if salt is a main ingredient in a potion or a request for Epsom salts. I mean, it's Hepa, so there's also the possibility that she was screeching at me that I'm a salty bitch and all I picked up was the one word.

Just then Frank bursts in through the bathroom door. I startle, sending a spray of saltwater across the heated tiles and accidentally crushing some of Roar's softer bits.

"Is this some new form of torture?" Roar asks.

"No, you idiots," Frank says. "It's me."

"Yes, Frank, we know it's you," I tell him, rising and wrapping a towel around myself, impressed that he doesn't even give me a once over. Things must be going quite well with his wife.

Frank shakes his head. "No. Guys. I'm not Frank."

"Then who are you?" Roar asks, about to come up out the tub with fists flying—and probably other things too.

"It's me—Helena!"

"You are clearly Frank," Roar says.

"You know that enchanted necklace that we used to impersonate Robert? Well..." Frank–no Helena–sweeps her hand up, lifting her collar so we can see. "I'm wearing it."

"You were only supposed to come in if something went really wrong!" I chide. "That was the plan!"

"You contacted Hepa with your mind. You asked her how to destroy the ring. Shit went wrong, Crystal," Helena shoots back.

"That...is..." I pause. "That's fair. But why..." I motion to her Frank disguise. "How did you know he was our guard?"

"Hepa again. She bugged everyone who works in this compound." Hepa specializes in tech magic. "Frank went home and confessed to his wife about everything that goes on here." Helena eyes me. "I'm sorry that you were tortured..."

"I wasn't!" I tell her quickly. "I mean, I was, but it wasn't really torture."

"What are you talking about?" Helena asks. "Frank thought he'd half-killed you."

"She can breathe underwater," Roar explains. "Her power is manifesting."

"Breathe underwater?" Helena asks, peering at me. "Like a fish? Do you have gills now?"

"No!" I blush. "Not that there's anything wrong with that, if I did. You've got goat horns, you know. I just, somehow, convince the water to give my lungs the oxygen."

"Well, regardless, I'm glad you weren't in any pain," Helena tells me. For Helena, that's like declaring her undying friendship. I rush forward and hug her. She leans in for a brief squeeze, then shakes me off, the smell of Frank's cologne surrounding us both.

"Wait," I pull back, my hands on her shoulders. "What did you do to Frank? You've got his ID and pass, so you can't tell me you just put on the necklace and waltzed in here. Is he lying somewhere concussed?" I try to give her a stern look, but Roar has come to his feet and Helena's attention is very diverted.

"Roar, could you please put on some pants?" I ask him.

Roar looks down then up at me. "Why?"

"Because we have company..." I motion to Helena.

"Don't mind me," she says. "Ford and I know that looking isn't cheating. Not for us, anyway. You can appreciate someone else's...form."

I snap. "Well, that is you and Ford. I would like you to back out of the bathroom now, and stop appreciating my..." I pause. I don't know what we are. "My Roar's dick."

Helena holds up her hands—Frank's hands. "Fine, it's not like I haven't seen it before." She turns her back on us...but is facing the mirror so we're both all clearly visible. I throw Roar a towel for his waist and then piece together what is left of my clothes, while Helena fills us in on what she knows. "Good job on jamming the cameras and mics in the bathroom. The security guys don't like it, but they're all too scared to come in here and investigate in case Roar goes off on them."

"They are wise," Roar mutters, sending a 'you see' look my way.

"So I, or well, Frank volunteered to come and take a looksy," Helena continues.

"Now, what about Frank?" I demand of Helena as I sit on the edge of the bathtub and start to brush out my hair. There are some huge snarls in it from all my ecstatic thrashing in the sheets…er, towels.

"Again, I didn't hurt Frank," Helena says." I would have, but he was remarkably easy to convince. He said was done being Busk's lackey. That he would devote his life now to the happiness of his wife. Some nonsense like that."

"Good for him," I say. "What about Busk?" I ask.

Roar leaves the bathroom and comes back a moment later, wearing a pair of pants, but shirtless. "If I ever get my powers back, I will rip that man in two."

"Yeah, he's got some serious tiny dick energy going on," Helena agrees. "But he found the decoy. And tonight he's going to attempt to use it to become a god."

"If Maddie's copy holds up to scrutiny, he'll try to use it to become a god. It won't work…but that just means he'll know he was tricked, and he'll still be on my tail."

"I have a message from Hepa. You wanted to destroy your piece?" Helena asks. "Are you sure?"

I shake my head no, but what I say is "Yes."

She raises her—Frank's—eyebrows at me.

"What I want is to prove myself worthy and to take my place with you and Maddie. But if that isn't going to happen then yes, I want to destroy it so Busk doesn't get it." Everything comes out in a rush, but even as I say it, I realize it's true.

"That's what I thought you would say. Hepa gave me the spell you'll need. It...basically takes the magic away from something. It might not even work on the *talentum*."

"We may have to try," I say. "But only as a plan B...or C...or whatever letter we're on then."

"The instructions are, and I quote, 'Sealed in salt, surrounded by air, salt and water, ADD MORE.'"

"Next order of business," Helena says, straightening her shoulders. "My instructions—as Frank—are to take you and Harmony to breakfast with Busk so he can gloat. He wants me to leave Roar here."

Roar steps forward to protest. "I will not leave Crystal's side. She has taken my seed."

Helena shakes her head. "You two finally boned? I mean, you were naked in the tub together but I didn't want to assume."

"Yes, we made love," I say.

"Good for you. I know it's only been like, a week since you met, but I'm surprised you two didn't get up to something at Roar's cabin."

"Crystal is mine..." Roar starts.

But I hold up a hand. "I *am* yours," I tell him. "But I'm not *just yours*. I'm not one thing. I need to do this and you can't come with me."

Roar sighs heavily, but then to my surprise, picks me up, plants a soft kiss on my head, and then sets me down again. "Take that with you for emotional support."

Touched, I press my hand to the kiss. "I will. Thank you."

Helena nods. "After breakfast he's going to take you and Harmony with him to the ceremony at the wharf, the one where he figures out the *talentum* we placed there is a fake."

"Okay, so then what do we do?" I ask.

"Pray he doesn't kill you on the spot," Helena says, turning when there's a sharp rap on the door. "I hope you're hungry. Busk says he likes to give you a good last meal."

19

———

At breakfast, my eggs are watery and I can only poke at them, watching the yolk spill out over the plate while Busk goes on about his plans for the future—of the entire world.

I'm trying to tune him out when Harmony is escorted to the table, her own guard pulling her chair out for her, then making sure she has everything she needs, including a just-the-right-temperature cup of tea. I wonder if she saw the benefit of my giving relationship advice to Frank and decided to befriend her own guard. But then Busk explains.

"Allow me to introduce my new Head of Magical Operations —your mom," he says, with an expansive sweep of his arm. "Believe me when I say that I think she found the contract quite satisfactory. She's got it in ink now that I won't drown you, among other things."

"Harmony!" I cry out, almost coming to my feet. "You can't work for this man!"

"I can't watch you almost die in front of me again, either," she shoots back. Then, in my head her voice says something else, quieter, calmer.

Your power saved you once. It can't save you from other things. Like chainsaws. Like fire. He has whole rooms, Crystal. For very special purposes. I got the complete tour last night and a long time alone to consider our options. This is for the best.

"This is such a depressing meal," Busk complains. "You guys are a bunch of wet blankets. No offense," he says, elbowing me in the side. I spit out the little bit of egg I'd managed to get into my mouth and glare at him.

"I propose a road trip," he goes on. "Who would like to go visit a very special place? You could even say it's the place where everything started, and the beginning of our story."

"I don't want to be in a story with you," I mutter into my plate.

"Too bad," he says, snapping his fingers to bring a guard to his side. "You're in it, and I'm calling the shots. Next stop, the wharf!"

We're all piled into a black-paneled van with leather seats and tinted windows that don't roll down. It's got restraining devices for its passengers instead of seat belts, but Busk doesn't insist that we be held. Helena, still disguised as Frank, follows us into the back. I'm confident Busk and the driver are listening to everything that is said in the back, so I reach out to Harmony mentally again.

What's going to happen?

He'll try the ceremony, she says. And it won't work. He'll know we tried to trick him and then...all bets are off. He won't kill you as long as he needs to find the real talentum, *but there is nothing in the contract I signed about not hurting you. Or your man.*

I have to protect him, I tell her, a sudden fear clenching my gut. I think of Roar strapped to the dunking board, powerless, being drowned right in front of me. I couldn't go through that. I'd give up the *talentum* before a hair on his head got wet.

You have to do what is right for more than just you. Harmony says sternly, as we pull into a familiar parking lot, with a charred stain in the middle of it where my ex-husband met his fiery death.

An entire fleet of black vans pulls in around us, and Helena hops out, keeping her gun on us as she continues to pretend to be Frank. Hordes of witches and warlocks pour out of the vans, forming a circle in the parking lot. Most of them have some kind of collar around their necks, while others are wearing mechanical wristbands.

It's to keep control of them, Harmony tells me, when she catches my glance. *They are tracked, but also it limits their powers. Busk is going for quantity over quality; all of their powers are dimmed so that no one person can launch a magical attack.*

She nods toward the guards, who are fully human, and locked and loaded. No matter how much magic is gathered in this circle, it would take a lot of coordination and communication to push back against Busk—and he's made sure they can't. Plus, if they try, they'll catch lead for their trouble. To make things worse, I see some witches moving through the group who aren't wearing a collar or a wristband; there are some who have come fully over to Busk, either for the paycheck, or the promise of power.

Either way, we can't expect any help from them.

"Frank, come here," Busk calls to Helena, who—even though she knows exactly how important her cover is—clearly has a hard time not just telling him to fuck off. She sighs and ducks her shoulders a little, like Frank would, before humbly walking over to her boss. Busk shows Frank something on his phone—probably a picture of the *talentum*—and sends him into the warehouse to retrieve it. Helena gives me an apologetic look over her shoulder as she goes into the building. Busk gives instructions and we all gather in a circle in the parking lot, the black smear that used to be my husband in the center.

"That's where Bobby died," I tell Harmony. She perks up for a second, walks over to the charred spot, scuffs her shoe over it, and then spits three times onto the pavement.

"He was incinerated on the spot, because the *talentum* found him unworthy," I say, loudly. "Just like what's going to happen here today."

I know it didn't deter him before, but hopefully the image of the black smear that used to be Bobby will give Busk pause. He only glances up from his phone, and shrugs.

"Your former husband didn't have a magical army. All he brought to the table was an ego and what he thought was knowledge of magical artifacts."

"He also had a hell of a crank on him," Helena adds, as she emerges from the building as Frank. Busk shoots her a look and Frank has the decency to blush. "I mean...you might not know this, boss, but the guy had a side gig in porn. Extramarital marriages weren't his only secrets."

Busk seems to accept this reasoning for Frank to know the size of Bobby's dick, and I shoot Helena a glance, but she only shrugs. For all I know, what she said is actually true. Leave it to Bobby to foist one more surprise on us from the grave.

"Finally," Busk says, taking the fake *talentum* from Helena. "All my dreams are about to be realized."

He nods to two other guards, who open the back of an armored vehicle and pull out two silver suitcases. Busk taps a code into each one and pulls out the other two pieces of the *talentum*—Maddie's, and Helena's. Frank's eyes go wide, and I can feel the pull inside of Helena at the sight of it.

That was hers.

Hers to keep.

Hers to protect.

And she lost it.

I shoot her a warning glance, hoping she'll catch it. Yes, she might have a gun, but I guarantee she doesn't know how to use an AR. Plus, even if she can figure out how to get the safety off, there's a dozen other armed goons who will take a shot at her before she can cap their boss. This is not the time to lose her infamous temper. She catches my glare, and her shoulders sink a little. Yes, it would probably feel amazing to gun Busk down in cold blood and in broad daylight. But there are too many risks.

She could use her powers, too. But I've not fully explored mine, and hers weren't powerful enough at Maddie's wedding to defeat Busk—and we had Maddie with us then. We still lost. I give a small shake of my head, and she nods, seeming to agree. Even with the powers we have between us, it's just the two of us against Busk and both his armies. We need to wait until all of us are together, and we know exactly what we are doing. Besides, we know he's not going to come into his powers at this moment, not when one of the *talentum* pieces is a phony.

The magical army—along with the human, armed one—forms a circle around the burnt section that used to be Bobby. Busk marches to the middle, carrying each piece of the *talentum*. He sinks to his knees, getting his designer pants dirty. He takes the three pieces of the *talentum* and begins to assemble them, while the witches start to chant and hum.

"It won't work!" I scream at Busk, still hoping for a distraction. "It won't accept you and you'll burn here today!"

He puts the globe that was given to Maddie into the base that was given to Helena. The fake giant stone ring is last, attached on top of the globe.

"Sing louder, will you?" Busk instructs, and the witches do his bidding.

What are we going to do? I ask Harmony. *He's going to figure out in like ten seconds that this isn't the real deal.*

Harmony, grim-faced, makes eye contact with me. *I've got an idea, but I can't say anything yet. Just work with me. And...try not to be too horrified.*

That does NOT sound good, but I don't have time to ask more, or wonder what horrible thing my usually love-and-peace-filled mother might be planning. Busk has finished his chant, and is kneeling in front of the complete *talentum*, hands held upward to the sky. The witches fall silent, the humans look upward, as if expecting a lightning bolt.

Nothing happens.

Busk sighs heavily, lets his arms fall to the ground. He says something in a foreign language once, loudly, shoving his hands back into the air. Again, nothing happens.

Except Busk throws a fit.

He yells, jumps to his feet, and starts kicking at the pieces. My fake stone ring files off to the left, where a warlock snags it from the air. A second kick hits Maddie's globe, but it's solid metal, a real piece of the *talentum*, and it fights back simply by being an inert object. Busk screeches in pain, now hopping on one foot and holding a two-thousand-dollar loafer in the other.

"Oh my god," I say, completely shocked by this, if nothing else the man has ever done. "That is quite the temper tantrum."

"Or should you say, *talentum* tantrum?" Helena asks, leaning in and raising an eyebrow. It's so ridiculous that I sputter a laugh, which is exactly the wrong thing to do. Busk glances up, enraged. He stalks over to us, limping and yelling instructions for his lackeys to gather the *talentum* pieces.

"Get in the van!" he yells at us. And while he is just a big, overgrown baby, he's also currently commanding both a magical army and a human one, so we do what we're told.

There's a lot of yelling in the van. The driver tries to keep a straight face while Busk slams the dashboard, screaming incoherently. His face is red and suffused with rage, his words a string of anger with no rationality. When he finally pulls himself together, he spins to us in the back.

"Why didn't it work?" he demands. "And don't give me that line about the *talentum* not choosing me. I didn't burn up. There was no negative magical energy for my witches to subvert. There was no magic at all. Why?"

Forgive me. Harmony thinks in my direction. *It's to protect you. I don't trust him.*

I don't trust him either, he's a megalomaniac, I say, confused as to why there's even a question of trusting Busk at this point.

Not Busk. Harmony says.

"Wait, what?" I ask, accidentally speaking aloud.

But it's too late.

"Because you needed a blood sacrifice," Harmony tells him. "You need an unwilling victim. You need to kill the berserker."

Roar.

20

When we get back to the compound Busk is still furious, but the rage has a direction and a purpose now—he's going to kill Roar.

My heart feels like it's can't decide whether to stop all motion or gallop right out of my chest. I think I might be having a panic attack. I can't decide which emotion to feel first—fear or fury. Or betrayal. Honestly, I know there are lots of crazy mother's out there, but how many of them try to get their daughter's boyfriend killed?

As soon as we're out of the van Busk motions for a guard to come over, and insists on having Roar brought to us. My hand clamps onto Helena's, terrified that Busk is going to dive in and perform the ceremony immediately, and Roar will die while Busk tries to make magic with a fake *talentum*.

"What the hell is wrong with you?" I hiss at Harmony, not even bothering to use telepathy. I'm so hurt and broken that I can't put the energy into it.

Harmony closes her eyes, like she's summoning the patience to deal with me and my annoying questions once again. "It's for the best, Crystal. I've felt the anger inside that man. And any second it's going to burst out of him, killing anyone who's in his path. I won't let that be you."

"I've felt his anger, too. And the pain. And I still love him!" I shriek at her, my voice rising to the roof of the vehicle bay, bouncing off all the shiny surfaces and high-end luxury vehicles.

"Daughter," Harmony says sternly, putting her hands on my shoulders. "Just because you love him does not mean he is good for you."

"He's not Bobby!" I yell, my eyes filling with tears. "He's different, special. *We're* special. We're supposed to be together, Mom. I just know it."

Her mouth goes into a flat line and she just stares at me. I know what she's thinking; this is the exact same fight we had about Bobby, and I practically said the same things then.

"This *is* the man you are supposed to be with," Harmony agrees, but her mouth is still tight and angry. "I saw it from the beginning that fate would bring you two together. But fate can be a cruel bitch, and the two of you together means your death."

"I accept that," I say, straightening my shoulders.

"I don't," she says, just as forcefully. "And so I've arranged for him to die. Plus, it will save us a little time."

"WHAT??!?!" It's Busk's turn to shriek, and all heads swivel toward him as he stalks back over to the group. "Frank," he yells, snapping his fingers. "You're the only loyal man in the group. It seems that the berserker has finally lost his mind while he was all alone and has destroyed half the room. If we're going to make this happen, I need that man in shackles, ready to die for me. Go get him and I'll give you five million dollars."

Frank goes white, and while I know that Busk surely thinks it's because he's a cowardly rent-a-cop, I know that it's actually Helena who just had all the blood run out of her face —and why.

She and Roar aren't exactly best friends; sparks tend to fly around them. If she walks into that room with a gun, and he rushes her, she might just shoot him. Or worse, her own powers will strike back in self-defense, and her identity will be revealed.

My throat closes, tears falling down my cheeks. Roar is alone, and scared. But he's also scary—and I'm the only one who can help him. Probably also the only one who is willing to do it.

"I'll go," I say, stepping forward. "I'll bring him to you."

"Crystal! No!" Harmony grabs my shoulder, but I shake her off.

"I'm the only one who can calm him," I explain to Busk. "I can do this. Let me talk to him."

"Ah, the adoring woman who wants one more moment alone with her lover," Busk smirks. "Charming."

He nods to Frank. "Take her to him."

"No!" Harmony shrieks and grabs at me, not letting me slip away this time. I grip her elbow, my hand running down the length of her arm. I squeeze her hand and for a moment I can tell that she thinks that she's won. That I've decided to let Roar rage, to let them kill him.

"Crystal..." she starts, her eyes searching mine. I wonder if she's going to apologize for all the times she made me feel like a child...way past the point where I wasn't one anymore. She doesn't have time because I find the ring on her finger, and yank. She yelps in surprise, backing away, and rubbing her hand.

I slip it on my own finger. The very piece of the *talentum* that Busk wants, which should be the size of a steering wheel. Harmony clutches at my hand, a warning in her eyes.

"Don't touch me!" I scream at her, partly for show, but there is real anger inside of me, too. Harmony doesn't get to decide who I am with. Harmony isn't Fate. She's just a human. And while she might be my mother, she doesn't get to make decisions for me anymore.

"Crystal!" she cries out, her voice in the air around us, but also in my head, scattered, and frantic. *He will kill you. He cannot help it. It's not his fault, but you will die.*

Then I die! I mentally scream back.

Do not try to destroy the talentum, *she warns. It is old power. Old magic. It will fight back and magic is not always kind.*

Neither are you, I shoot back, and slam the door behind me as Helena leads me to the room that Roar and I share.

There are holes in the drywall of the hallway. As we pass, an arm shoots out of one and grabs Frank's ankle. Helena goes down, but spins and cracks Roar's wrist with the butt of the rifle. He screams in pain and the muscular arm disappears, only to be followed by the sound of a piece of furniture crashing against the wall. I grab Helena and pull her to her feet. She's visibly shaken and pale, sweat running down her face.

"Harmony might be right," she tells me. "He's out of his mind. I'm not sure I can let you go in there."

"It's not up to you," I tell her, and snatch Frank's ID card from her lanyard. I scan it on the panel next to the door and toss it back in her shocked face as I step through the doorway.

I slam the door behind me. Roar turns to me, sweaty and naked, all of his muscles taut. His eyes are white, his mouth drawn into a snarl.

"It's me!" I scream, my back against the wall, both arms in front of me—either in defense or appeal, I don't know. "Roar! I'm yours!"

Throwing his head back he bellows his ear-shattering berserker battle cry.

I'm guessing it's going to take more than just a simple declaration. All right, then. It's not like I expected this to be easy. I hoped, but I didn't expect.

Now I quickly strip naked. I figure it's best to meet Roar in my most natural state. Also, he made it clear that he liked my boobs, so if all else fails maybe they'll bring him back to himself.

As if waiting to meet an opponent, Roar stays in the same spot, watching me while keeping his weight balanced forward, ready to charge.

"I LOVE YOU!" I bellow at him, trying to reach the same volume as his berserker cry. I don't get even close...not with my vocal cords. But I manage to tap into the part of me that can reach out to him and feel what he's feeling.

Suddenly, I can feel the hot thud of his blood and the tension that can only be released by attacking, breaking, and destroying everything he sees.

Oh, Roar. My heart cries for him to be caught up like this, kinda like waking up in the worst mood ever and not being able to shake it—but times a million.

Still, beneath all that, once I dig deep inside him, my Roar is still there. And he's struggling to get free.

"Roar!" I yell his name running at him with my arms flung open as wide as they'll go.

For a moment he seems stunned. Maybe by the bounce of my boobs. But it's enough time for me to fling myself into his arms and suction my body to his. I wrap all my limbs around him, clinging like a koala to its favorite eucalyptus tree.

"You're mine, and I'm yours, and I am not letting you go."

Roar growls and one his hands comes up the back of my neck to knot itself in my hair. I'd tucked my face into the hollow of his neck, but he jerks the fistful of hair so that my head is forced back. With a twist of his wrist he could snap my neck, but instead he just looks down at me.

"Baby..." I whisper. "I know you're in there."

"You're...mine?" He leans in and sniffs at me. His grip tightens just a fraction and I stare into his eyes, my chest heaving.

"Mine?" he asks, growling. Confusion clouds his eyes and he drops his hand from my hair and tries to shake me off. I manage to hold on, which means he's not really trying all that hard.

"Yes! And you're mine!" I shout at him. "My heart belongs to you."

"I belong to you." Finally, it's not a question. "Crystal?"

There's a fierce look on his face, but I'm not scared. He wraps his arms around me and once again, I become one with him, but not just our minds. In our souls. I don't see his memory but I do see the same darkness that I did before.

I reach out and I soothe his dragon heart, while pressing kisses to every bit of him that I can reach.

"Crystal," he says, and I can feel his hot tears as they drip from his face. "I almost killed you."

"But you didn't," I soothe him. I unwrap my legs, because they're getting tired, but Roar's arms come around me so that our bodies are still pressed together. So that we are one.

I press my forehead to his. Then press a soft kiss to his lips.

"You don't have to be afraid of your beast anymore," I tell him. "I collared it and tagged it. That wyvern belongs to me."

Roar's eyes widen and then, at last, a smile enters them. "I am your berserker now."

"Yes," I agree. "And I am yours...whatever I am."

"You will be my woman for now and forever," Roar states. "I pledge on my Viking honor."

"You will be my man for now and forever," I repeat his words, having a feeling they're more than just sweet nothings but a sort of handfasting ceremony. "I pledge on my honor."

Roar sighs deeply as if some great weight has been lifted from him. "Now we will complete the pledge with our bodies." He turns me so that back is to a wall. "Next time," he promises, "We will have a bed."

"A bed? Please." My hand slides down Roar's body until I find his cock ready and waiting for me. "All I need is this."

21

I'm pulling away from Roar, and wiping down my body from the sweat and...other things, when there's a very loud cracking noise. A black scar has opened on the opposite wall, and I shoot Roar a questioning glance.

"I didn't do that one," he says, just as the crack starts to smoke and steam.

"Oh, shit!" I scream. "There's a fire!"

Roar jumps to his feet and stands in front of me, as if his body can shield me from flames. I know it can't, but I still appreciate the gesture. At my cry, the door busts open and Helena comes rushing in, Frank's rifle at the ready.

But she doesn't need to use it, because it's not a fire, and there's no enemy to fight. The crack widens, some flames spitting out—but they're not dangerous, because the wall isn't on fire. They're coming from Aden, as he pushes through the wall, out of an actual portal to Hell.

"Thank Hades," he says, as he steps into the room. "Ford's map worked!" He reaches behind him and helps Maddie into the room. She steps lightly over the burning ledge, all smiles and grace.

"Knock knock!" she says.

I rush to her. "I am so glad to see you," I say. "Except..." I'm about to tell her that we're most certainly under surveillance. I might be able to fog things up in the bathroom, but we're out in the living area now, and while Ford's map might have led them straight to us, he had no way of knowing he's just walking into a cell—and a monitored one, at that.

But I don't have time to say these things. Maddie embraces me and gives my back a good rub. Such a mom thing to do... well, not a thing *my* mom would do. My mom would kick my shin and tell me that I did a stupid thing, then maybe follow it up with some chamomile tea and an aura cleanse.

Ford steps in behind her and his gaze sweeps the room, no doubt looking for Helena.

"Oh, no!" I cry, just as I see Aden has spotted Frank—and his gun. Aden raises hands, undoubtedly getting ready to hit Helena with duel fireballs.

"Wait!" she cries, dropping the gun and yanking the necklace off. Frank is immediately gone, with tall, lithe Helena taking his place.

The fire dies in Aden's hands. "Sorry, for a second I forgot you're in disguise."

"Babe!" Ford cries and sweeps her into his arms.

Aden turns his attention back to the portal, which is growing smaller and smaller. Sweating and clearly over-worked at the effort it took to open it, his handsome face contorts as he groans.

"We should leave now; I can't keep this open for much longer."

"I can't leave," I say. "Not without Harmony."

"Then throw the ring in, like it's freaking Mordor!" Ford says. "See if Busk can find it in hell!"

I rush forward the ring off my finger, but I hesitate a little too long and the portal closes. I touch the wall. It's cool to the touch. There's no char, no ashes or embers. That is definitely impressive.

He collapses to the floor and Maddie kneels beside him. "Are you okay?"

"That took a lot out of me," he admits. Aden is a big guy, strong and well-muscled. He's also a demi-god. You can tell he's not used to feeling weak. I glance at Roar, wondering if he can offer some sort of man-assistance in the arena of losing your mojo. Maybe offer some encouraging words, but he doesn't offer any.

"Will you be able to open a portal for us to leave?" Helena asks unabashedly.

"Give him a moment to recover," I chide.

"Opening the portal wasn't easy for him," Maddie agrees.

"No, it's okay." Aden climbs to his feet. "Let me try..." He raises his hands and makes a gasping noise. Then a long groan escapes him. The portal sputters open, the size of a basketball, but again, before I can throw the ring through it collapses in on itself.

"Shit," Helena says what we're all thinking.

"There goes our rescue attempt," Aden mutters, looking up at Maddie sheepishly.

She touches his face, which looks hot enough to burn. But Maddie doesn't flinch. "We knew this was a possibility. When we found out this place was underwater, you told us that you might not be able to portal everyone out."

"It's still a bit of a kick to the ovaries," Helena says.

"We'll just fight our way out," Roar says.

"Or sit tight," Maddie offers. "Let Aden rest up."

"We can't," I tell them. "I'm confident this room is monitored, and he'll be busting in here any second. Not all of his goons will flip to our side as easy as Frank did. And if he finds the *talentum* we're done. He has an army of witches working for him. He won't have to prove himself worthy or wait for his powers. He'll be a god."

We all eye each other. "So what should we do?" Ford asks.

I clear my throat. "We need to destroy my piece of the *talentum*.

Helena, always the pragmatist, says. "I'm with you, Crystal."

"Me too," Maddie agrees. Aden steps behind her, while Ford sidles up to Helena. I turn to find Roar at my back. A good man knows when to support his woman.

"Let's do this!" I say, pulling Harmony's ring from my finger and setting it on the floor.

"How?" Maddie asks, a perfectly straight line forming above her nose.

"Salt," Roar and I say together.

"It's a magical deterrent," I explain. "And luckily the bathroom has a saltwater tap. My powers came in while I was down here, and I can communicate with water. If I ask the seawater to attack the ring with its salt elements, this just might work."

"Might as well," Helena says, with a shrug.

"Give a try, girl!" Maddie agrees.

I tell everyone to back up and I sit, cross-legged on the floor. Roar goes into the bathroom and turns on the salt tap. I let the sound of the running water fill my ears, and I reach out towards it.

Hello,

Hello, it answers, clearly happy to have someone to talk to again.

I need something, and I'm sorry I'm always asking, never giving anything. My friends and I are in a lot of trouble, and we need help. I promise if you step in, we'll all donate some money to Save the Whales, or something.

The water is quiet for a second, probably wondering why it got such an idiot as its magical ambassador.

Environmental Defense Fund.

Oh, I hadn't expected that. The water is haggling with me.

Yes! Whatever you want!

Agreed. What is it that you need?

I explain my idea about the salt molecules attacking the *talentum*, hopefully destroying its magical properties. The water makes no promises, but a snake of tap water emerges from the bathroom, reaching its soggy tentacle out into the bedroom.

"Wow!" Maddie says. "Crystal, your power is so cool!"

I don't respond. I need to concentrate, but I can hear murmurs from the others as well. The water tentacle hovers over the ring for a moment, then envelops it, lifting the small circle of metal into the air. For a moment it changes colors, seems to rust at an advanced rate, the smooth surface becoming pock-marked, pieces of rust flaking off.

"Is it working?" Maddie asks.

"I...I don't know..." I say. The ring stays suspended in the water, spinning as it's attacked by the salt molecules.

"Something's happening," Helena says.

I wonder if it will go up in smoke, or just disappear, perhaps melt into a puddle of non-magical metal. Or maybe it will explode. My piece of the *talentum*. And it *is* mine. My destiny.

For almost a year, I've waited patiently to claim my powers. To join Helena and Maddie. And now that will never happen. I'm making a choice, and while I know it's the right thing to do, I still feel a tug of doubt—*did I make the right decision?*

Regret fills me as the ring starts to shake and then spin. It's getting bigger and I fear that it *will* explode. Roar puts his bulk in front of me, but I push past him, not willing to let him catch the literal flak if the shit hits this particular magical fan. But the water is weakening, the tentacle becoming smaller and less robust. The ring stops spinning, and the rust recedes, the shining, smooth metal taking its place.

It is too strong, the water tells me.

"Oh no," I say, realizing what's happening. This isn't the goal, isn't what I wanted. In fact, it's the complete opposite.

The ring is getting bigger, growing to its true size. It's no longer small enough to put on my finger and pretend it's a chunky fashion choice. It grows to the size of a steering wheel and gives one last shudder.

Attacking it with salt water didn't destroy it; it returned it to its normal state.

The water evaporates into a mist, and the full sized *talentum* falls to the floor with a clang.

We all stare at it.

"We didn't destroy it," Maddie says.

"No," Helena catches on. "We destroyed the magic that was keeping it small."

"Is there any possible way that Busk doesn't find out about this?" I ask.

"No," Busk's voice comes over a speaker. "There isn't."

22

"Well, that was quite the show." Busk's voice is so arrogant I can just imagine the smirk on his face. "This has been immensely helpful."

Then I don't have to imagine because Busk's face appears on the wall, which apparently is a video screen. "Hello everyone, so good to see you all again."

"Rat bastard," Helena says and tries to open the door. "It's locked," she tells us.

"Now, don't be like that. I know it's hard to be on the losing end. Well, actually, I don't. I've never lost. But I'm sure it's a horrible feeling. Now that I'm about to have all three pieces of the *talentum*—the real ones, Crystal, you sneaky girl—I will have all the assurance I need to make sure I never lose, ever."

Roar looks at Busk's image. "Come and get it," he says, cracking his knuckles.

Busk laughs. "I have people for that."

The door opens and Frank—the real Frank—steps through. He's been beaten up, and he has a fresh black eye.

"I'm sorry," he tells us. "If I don't retrieve that"—he points to the *talentum*—"Busk is going to kill my wife."

"It's one life," Helena says. "And from the sounds of it, a life that only recently saw any type of improvement. I mean, really, did you get a vibe check? Maybe she's cool with dying."

"Helena!" Maddie chides.

"What? It's true," Helena says, throwing her hands in the air. "If it takes one life to get the better of Busk, it's worth it."

"It won't be one life," Frank says. "Because I will die fighting to save my Bethany."

Roar steps forward to accept the challenge but I put a hand on his arm. "Enough. We're not going to become Busk. We're not going to sacrifice innocent people."

I pick up the now huge, heavy ring and lug it over to Frank. He looks at me with his wet eyes. "I really am sorry," he says.

"It's okay," I tell him. "You're doing this in the name of love. How can I hold that against you?"

He backs away, probably getting the feeling that the tide could turn at any moment and Roar might not share my Meatloaf mentality.

He runs out the door; it closes behind him, locking us in.

"Great, now we're trapped with no weapons and no *talentum*," Helena says.

Harmony's voice comes seering into my brain, screeching.

Busk, the son of a bitch, is here gloating. You're all a bunch of demigods and goddesses! Do something!

I roll my eyes. Leave it to Harmony to make us feel bad when we're already down. "Harmony wants to know why we don't just badass our way out of here?"

"My powers are tamed," Roar says. "I might be able to get through the door if I get very angry, but I can't promise anyone's safety but Crystal's."

"Okay, don't want to die," Maddie says. "Next. Aden, babe, any mojo?"

"Unfortunately, as we've seen, my powers underwater are dampened—no pun intended," Aden says. He opens one hand as if to create a fireball, but only a puff of smoke emerges.

"There's no dirt for me to use..." Helena says. "Maybe I could use the seafloor and raise it. But it might be catastrophic for the environment, plus we'd all drown. Except Crystal, apparently, but I'm not sure how useful she would be solo."

"I could...try to seduce Busk, I guess," Ford says.

Helena shakes her head. "Let's not go there."

"You don't think I could?" he asks.

"Oh, I know you could. But I'm not pimping you out." Helena tells him.

"Awww, you guys are so sweet," Maddie says. Helena rolls her eyes, but Maddie continues, "I'm not sure how my powers can help us either."

"It's so adorable watching all of you debate how to defeat me, when you are absolutely and totally at my disposal," Busk's voice is piped into the room, the video of his pale, shiny face no longer there for us to direct our hate at.

"But unfortunately, I have something I need to do, and I can't risk all of you half-assed gods and homemakers getting in my way. It's been fun, cute couples, but I'm afraid it's time for me to make my grand exit. And you're not coming along. Well...not all of you."

"You can't have Roar!" I scream, jumping in front of him. I put my arms out, circling his body, not sure where to expect an attack from, but absolutely confident that one is coming.

Crystal, listen to me. Harmony's voice is strident in my head, powerful.

"Silly Crystal," Busk says. "A better opportunity has provided itself."

"What do you mean?" I ask, arms still spread wide, muscles quivering.

I've volunteered to be the sacrifice.

"NO!" I scream, and everyone in the room stiffens, looking for a threat.

"Your mother has kindly offered herself in place of your man. I think there's some kind of making up for lost time angle going on there, or an apology for being kind of a crap mom your whole life—"

"She was never a crap mom!" I scream, directing my voice nowhere and everywhere.

"Well, she wasn't the *best* mom," Busk argues.

"Maybe not for someone else," I say, tears streaming down my face. "But she was the best mom for *me!*"

And I realize it's true. All the times Harmony made me question myself, or wonder if I was making the right choices weren't to undermine me, or make me feel bad, she was making me think hard, analyze the situation, weigh the pros and cons.

Harmony didn't want me reacting emotionally, because my emotions can be overwhelming. I let them flow through me and supersede everything else, even logic. Like right now, I'm still spinning around Roar, trying to protect him from an unseen danger, acting on emotion, when the truth is... there's nothing I can do. I step away from him, my arms falling to my sides.

Don't do this, I think toward Harmony. *Don't make me do life alone.*

You won't be alone, Crystal. Look around you.

I do, taking in not only Roar, but also Maddie and Helena. They're not just my sister-wives, like we used to joke. They're my honest to god sisters. They came here for me, and I fought for them. We're bound together, and our men with us. Ford and Aden didn't have to involve themselves either, but they chose to, because they love their wives—and that love extends to me.

"We're a family," I say out loud, my voice stronger now. "And we're going to fight like one."

"No," Busk says, his voice cold and flat. "You're going to die like one."

A vent pops open in the ceiling and we all jump. Ford goes to Helena, wrapping his arms around her, while Aden steps in front of Maddie, looking defiantly at the ceiling, ready for anything. Roar's arms encircle my waist, pulling me back toward him. There's a hissing sound and a gas starts to seep out of the vent; white and thick, it reaches for us, forming fingers and hands. Whatever this is, it's got some magic behind it.

Maddie screams and dives for the bed, grabbing pillows and blankets and shoving them into everyone's hands. Everyone else covers their faces, but I don't. I use all my energy and reach out to Harmony one last time.

I'm doing to die, Mom. You don't have to make this sacrifice.

There's a smell in the air, like cherries and vanilla, and I feel a tingling sensation across my whole body. My knees go weak and I slide to the floor, fighting to keep my eyes open.

Even if there's a sliver of a chance for you to live, and to be happy, I will die for that chance. Harmony says. *I've tried to protect you for your whole life. It's time for me to exit. It's time for me to trust that to Roar—and to you.*

"Nooo," I moan, but the gas fills my lungs and my eyes slide shut.

The last thing I see is Roar on the ground next to me, reaching for me, as the pulse in his neck starts to slow.

23

———

I'm being dragged. There are fingers digging into my armpits and it hurts, with pressure in all the wrong places. Not to mention my ass hitting every single stair as I'm taken...where!?! I come into consciousness thrashing, fighting, ready to kill or die—whichever one needs to happen in order to protect the people I love.

"Hey, woah! Hey!" It's Frank's voice, but that doesn't make me feel much better. He willingly followed Busk's orders about bringing him the real *talentum*, and while I can forgive him doing it for the sake of keeping his wife safe, that also means he's willing to do anything for her to stay that way.

"Don't touch me!" I shriek, pulling away from him. My head is fuzzy, and my mouth dry. I huddle in a corner of the stairwell, as Frank turns and heads back up the stairs. I doze off again and when I wake up Helena and Maddie are also propped against the wall, eyelids heavy as they come around.

And Frank is back as well. I fix him with a baleful glare.

"I'm not the bad guy here!" Frank cries out, holding his hands up in the air. "I couldn't just watch you guys die in there. Busk took off with your mom for the transportation hangar, and I slipped away. I didn't know if I'd be able to get you all out in time."

"You didn't!" I say, my throat closing. "Where are the men?"

Frank holds out his hands in supplication. "I opened the door and turned on the fan. I'm doing everything I can but I'm only one guy and I'm not in the best shape. I don't even know if I can move two of those dudes, the hell guy and your crazy man."

"I'll help," Helena says, coming to her feet shakily. "Wow, I feel..."

"Woozy," Maddie finishes for her, brushing hair out of her eyes as she rests her head against the stairwell. "And...empty?"

"It's the gas," Frank nods. "It's made to suck out your powers, temporarily taking away your magical mojo, then after longer exposure, kill your regular, human body."

"Buddy, this body ain't so regular," Helena says, flexing to prove her point. She's always been a workout queen, and her muscles are taut and defined. "Now, take me back to the room and let's move those hunks of male meat."

"You two" She spins on me and Maddie. "You figure out what our next move is. And make it fucking good."

I crawl over to Maddie, rest my head on her shoulder. She's right; I might not have had my powers for very long, but I do feel an emptiness inside of me where they have been dimmed. And I hadn't even fully communed with the *talentum*, like my sisters have. I can't imagine the loss she feels right now.

"It's still there," she says, rubbing her belly. "They're just quiet right now, unconscious. It's like when you're pregnant and the baby sleeps; it's still there, it's just not fully present and awake."

"I'll have to take your word for that," I say, patting my own flat belly.

Frank and Helena come back with Ford draped between them, his breaths coming heavily, but his eyes wide open.

"I swear I only grabbed him first because he was closest," Helena says, shooting us an apologetic look as she and Frank head back for Aden and Roar.

"What are we going to do?" I ask Maddie. "If we've all been zapped of our powers for who knows how long, how can we possibly fight Busk? And Harmony is going to..."

My voice drifts off. I can't speak about what Harmony is willing to do in order for me to be happy. She's willing to die in Roar's place, even if it only buys us a couple more hours together.

"Got your lug!" Helena announces, as she unceremoniously drops Aden to the ground in front of Maddie. She immediately goes to him, cradling his head in her lap, running her fingers through his hair. It's all very sweet, but all I can think about is the fading of Roar's pulse in his neck, and why the heck Helena is getting him *last*. I struggle to my feet, and try to climb the stairs, but my knees buckle after only three steps. The door at the landing busts open, and suddenly Roar is there. He's not outlined in fire, and his muscles aren't bulging...his eyes are normal, and he kind of looks like he's about to puke. But I don't care. All I know is that he's alive, he's moving, and he loves me.

We meet on the stairs, him stumbling down a few steps to end up next to me on all fours. I lurch into him, and both of us lose our balance. We end up pressed against the metal railing, heaving for breath, arms around each other, thankful to be alive.

"I love you," we both say at the same time. It's silly and they are just words, but I feel a quiver in my stomach, down where I can feel my powers move...among other things. I guess it's not that odd to believe that sexual desire, magic, and strength can all come from the same source.

"I'm sorry, I shouldn't have let it go so far," Frank says, finally done rescuing people. He's collapsed against the door, his back to it as each of us couples check each other for vital signs.

"It's okay, I'm going to murder you and we'll be even," Helena says, shooting him a glare.

"She doesn't mean that!" Maddie says. "It's fine. You did the right thing in the end."

I do agree that Frank eventually made the right choice, and I'm all for forgiving him, but I am definitely not on board with Maddie, thinking that everything is fine. Busk has all the pieces of the *talentum*, and he's going to kill my mom during a magical ceremony to take over the world. Deep down inside, I feel the quiver again.

I spin on Frank. "You said Busk had Harmony and was going to the transportation hangar, right?"

"Yeah," he nods, wiping the sweat from his brow. Everyone struggles to their feet, but I'm the one in the lead when we round on Frank.

"Tell us how to get there."

———

Ford drives a Jeep through a lush artificial jungle of plants and trees, following the signs with arrows and a big blue H.

"I don't need a hospital," Roar says.

"It's for a helipad," Ford tells him. "A helicopter. Busk must have all kinds of toys in his man cave."

We pull up to the hangar just in time to see a private jet being bussed out. All six of us pile out of the Jeep, and I sprint toward Harmony when I see her coming out of the hangar, led by Busk.

"You son of a bitch!" I scream, and I can feel the anger and the power in my belly swelling, filling me. Whatever magical dimming spell was in the gas, it's out of my system now. Frank pulled me out first, so the others might not be fully recovered, but I am.

And I'm pissed.

Busk actually pulls Harmony in front of him, using her as a shield.

Drop, I think directly at her. And she does. Harmony goes limp like a toddler having a fit and falls through Busk's arms onto the pavement. I hear the others yelling behind me, and footfalls as they rush to keep up. But I am a woman protecting her family, and no one can keep up with me.

Busk is expecting a magical attack, and so he's signaling for a witch to come to his aid when I punch him in the face. He goes down, blood spilling from his nose. He pulls his hand away and looks at it, shocked at the sight.

"You bastard!" I scream, kicking him while he's still down. He rolls onto his side, and looks up at me, smiling through the blood.

"How the hell do you keep staying alive?" he asks, genuinely curious. "Can I bottle whatever this is? Sell it? Would you be willing to do a thirty-second audio spot?"

"AAAHAHHH!!!" I scream, and haul back for another punch. But there's something stronger in me, in my gut, and I can feel it asking to be let out.

Hello.

It's not water molecules, but something different, like the actual power inside of me is speaking to me now.

Hello?

The human body is sixty percent water.

Huh? I look around, wondering where the Encyclopedia Britannica bot is. The others gather around me, looking down at Busk, who has come to his knees, still smiling. The witch he had been beckoning is approaching hesitantly, not entirely sure who has the upper hand here. The guard who follows her is armed, and seems to be keeping her in line.

"Not interested in selling out?" Busk asks. "Are you sure? I can make a mint off you guys… and of course a generous cut for each of you. I'm imagining a reality TV show, magical couples at home. Maddie can show off her kitchen skills, and Helena can have a cardio workout hour. Crystal, I'm not entirely clear on what you're good for, but we'll come up with something."

"The human body is sixty percent water," I tell him, suddenly aware of what the power wants me to do.

Busk pulls a face. "I don't know if a TV show about random facts is—"

His joke is cut short, his face suddenly tightening, along with the feeling in my stomach. It's like a belt pulling tighter around my waist, comfortable and then snug, tight and then pinching, as I allow it to flow. I reach out into Busk, feeling for the water in his body, each molecule, safely tucked into wet tissues and warm spots. Places that are kept entirely safe by armies of witches and warlocks, bullets and bad guys.

But it's not safe from me.

Hello?

All the water in his body reaches out to me, interested. I don't bother with a greeting.

Come here, I say sternly.

And Busk begins to wither.

24

I t starts with tears flowing from his eyes. He reaches up to touch them, clearly stunned. "What...?" he asks as he wipes away the wetness.

Next, droplets break out on his skin and sweat pours down his face. His expensive clothing immediately becomes soaked, his armpits drenched and the stain growing by the second.

Real worry starts to spread across his face.

"Guard!" he yells, no longer so confident. "Shoot her!" He points at me.

Fortunately we're above the water and Aden has regained enough of his powers to produce a small fireball in his hands. Its look alone deters the guard to slow down.

"You don't have to follow him. He's horrible," I tell them.

"I pay your wages," Busk barks dryly at them. "I provide for you."

"Not enough," the guard says.

Another one pipes up. "You barely pay minimum wage. And you don't offer dental."

The first one nods. "Yeah, I got three kids who are gonna need braces." He backs away. "I'm done with this shit. I'm gonna go work for my father-in-law at his landscaping business." He trots away.

The other two look at each other.

"Frank was right."

"This ain't worth it." They also turn tail and run.

"You should have offered dental," I tell Busk.

Busk has started to look noticeably parched, the skin on his face and hands flaking off. "Ungrateful! It's men like me who make the world go 'round. Without me..."

"The world would grind to a stop?" I ask, incredulously. "You really think that, don't you?" Busk has every privilege that money can buy, but the world doesn't need him. "No one needs you," I spit at him.

"You," he orders his team of magic wielders. "Take care of her, you useless hacks!"

One witch steps forward, tugging the collar at her neck. "We can't stop her. She's too powerful. You've put a dampener on us, remember? It was part of our contract." Several of the other witches agree, nodding their heads.

Busk reaches a shriveling hand into his sweat-soaked jacket and pulls out his phone. He drops it to the ground and falls to his knees after it.

He frantically types in a code and all the witch's collars vibrate, then pop open. A pattering follows as the tech falls to the pavement. "Now," Busk rasps. "Kill her."

The witch who spoke up hesitates for just a moment. She looks at Busk's desiccating form and back to me. I don't say anything. The people around Busk, they know how he is. They know who he is. I can see it in the eyes of this witch; Busk disgusts her.

"Consider this my resignation," she tells him, and turns on her heel. The other witches take the opportunity to cut and run as well, disappearing around the side of the hangar.

Busk writhes on the ground as the water in his body continues to abandon him. The small drops pool on the tarmac in front of him. They crawl toward me, called by my power. They form a puddle at my feet, waiting for further instruction. All water is mine to command.

Busk writhes, kicking in pain as I pull everything from him, his muscles shortening as they wither, pulling his body up into the fetal position.

"Stop!" he yells. "Please!" he adds, uncertain. It comes out awkwardly, a word he hasn't said in a long time.

I don't stop, don't even consider his plea. I reach deeper with my power, looking for more water, searching for every bit of liquid inside of him so that I can yank it out. His heart calls, full and juicy, so I turn my attention there.

Crystal, do you understand now? Water is life.

It's the voice that told me about the water. It's...the *talentum*.

I mentally gulp. *Yes? I understand? Um...thank you? And also... sorry for trying to destroy my piece. I didn't want to. I really really didn't want to. I've been so excited to get my powers, but I couldn't let Busk get this last piece.*

I don't think the *talentum* was expecting such a word vomit response. For a long moment it says nothing. Then, finally, *You cannot destroy an ancient power. You are lucky to be alive.*

I wince. *Yeah, that's what Harmony—um, my mother—told me. I guess I should've listened. Thanks for not killing me.*

You were saved by the medallion mark of protection, it tells me.

The...what? But then I remember. When I was just a baby my mom gave me a tattoo on my lower back. Yeah, a tramp stamp on a baby. Hard to rock a Disney princess bikini in the paddle pool when you're sporting that kind of ink at three years old. Harmony told me that she'd had a vision that it would come in handy someday. I guess today was that day.

Now, the *talentum* says. With that one word it's like the *talentum* just yelled out roll call for every drop of water in the universe and they all answered in unison: *HERE!*

There is so much water. Not just the oceans and lakes, but in every one of us and in plants and underground. Yes, water is life. And I am water. I am life. I am—

No, I tell the *talentum.* Because I already know from Maddie and Helena what comes next. This is my chance to take hold of ultimate power, to be the force of water itself. But to do that I'd have to leave my human body behind.

It's not tempting. Not even for a millisecond.

That type of power is not what I'm looking for, I tell the *talentum*. *I just want to be worthy of the little bit you already granted me through my Cancer sign.*

Yes, you are worthy, the *talentum* answers in a voice that sounds a little...snappish? Maybe I should've let it give me the whole ultimate power tour before turning it down.

Before I can apologize, I can feel the *talentum* leaving me.

Just like that I'm out of my head and back in the same instant I was before the *talentum* decided to have a little chat with me.

Busk gasps before me. The bastard who almost killed my Roar and then snagged my mother instead. He can never again threaten the people I love. Never.

There's a hand on my shoulder, someone trying to break my concentration. I shake them off, and dive back in, dedicated to wringing Busk out like dishrag.

Crystal, no. Don't do this. It's Harmony's voice, reaching into my head, begging. *You don't want to be like Busk. You're better than him. You don't want the weight of a death on your shoulders.*

I don't answer her, but I keep pushing, delving further into Busk, ready to extinguish his life like a bucket of water poured on a candle.

Suddenly, there's a different touch, heavy and warm, hands on my hips, a stubbled jaw against my neck, a rough voice in my ear.

"This is not you," Roar tells me.

I shake my head, crying now, fighting to find the last piece of life inside of this horrible man so I can kill it.

"I know death," Roar goes on, pulling me back against him, even as I struggle. "I know what it can do to a person, and I know that you will not be my Crystal any longer if you do this."

He's right. Harmony says. *And I don't want you to be the real sacrifice.*

I cry out, and break the connection between me and Busk. The pools of water shimmering at my feet immediately rush back into him, my hold over them broken.

Busk recovers amazingly fast as tears stream back into his eyeballs, sweat seeps into his skin. His skin tightens, his color comes back, and he rises to his knees and looks at me.

I expect to see anger.

But there's no rage there. Instead I'm met with astonishment.

Astonishment and...fear.

Busk is afraid of me.

But I don't have time to relish the feeling of power. Instead, I feel sick. I never wanted to become a thing of terror. Roar pulled me back from the edge. And Harmony. I would not have been able to live with myself if I'd killed Busk.

Everyone is here now, Maddie and Aden, Ford and Helena, and Roar. My Roar.

Fully recovered, Busk runs for the private jet. He takes the stairs two at a time, and he disappears into the carriage, the door closes behind them.

"Can we stop it?" Helena asks.

"Honey?" Aden looks at Maddie. "Can you use your air powers?"

Her forehead is crinkled in concentration. A wind whips up around us. All of her focus is bent on summoning her powers and the wind to stop the plane from taking off.

"I can't," she shakes her head. "That gas zapped me, and I'm not recovered yet."

The jet roars to life, speeding past us and knocking us all backwards as it takes to the air. Geoff Busk flies away, with all three pieces of the *talentum*—and more determined than ever to turn into a god, now that I've seen inside his heart, and I know who he truly is.

A scared little kid.

25

———

"So now what?" Helena asks as we pile into the helicopter we commandeered from Busk's personal fleet.

"Now we fly," Ford says, slipping into the pilot seat with a smile like that of a little boy on Christmas day.

Helena takes the co-pilot seat and gives him a good swat. "Obviously, and stop looking so pleased with yourself. We may be flying to our doom."

"No way," Aden says. "We're going to kick Busk's ass." He adds something else but it's lost as Ford turns on the helicopter and the whipping blades start to whirr with deafening force.

Ford holds up his pair of headphones and indicates we should all put ours on. I settle into a seat with Roar on one side and Harmony on the other. Maddie and Aden buckle in opposite us. As the helicopter takes to the air, we all put our headsets on and resume our conversation.

"As I was saying," Aden's voice is the first to come through the headphones. "We can take Busk."

"Even if he's a god?" Maddie asks.

"Look," Helena interrupts. "I refuse to fight this guy to a draw again. We need to take him down once and for all."

"I agree," Maddie says. "It's really hard to schedule activities for the kids when I don't know when I'll have to run off and fight a villainous billionaire."

"We men will kill him," Roar says, simply.

"Easier said than done," Harmony snaps. "I've never seen a man so warded up with protection spells. And that's not even taking into account all the witches he surrounds himself with. He's made himself into a cockroach; I don't even know if a nuclear bomb would take him out."

"We're not killing him," I say. "Did you guys all just miss the part where he was nearly a shrunken head? There has to be another way."

Everyone goes quiet at this. It's a bummer to know we're going after an unbeatable enemy. Except...

"What if we talked to the *talentum*?" I offer.

Helena turns around in her seat to shake her head at me. "Sure, we'll ask the magical object to help us out."

"Well, why not?" I say, feeling a little annoyed with her dismissive tone. "It's more than just a mindless thing. It chose us. It gave us powers and offered to make each one of us the gods of gods."

"And we turned it down," Maddie reminds me. "It might not want to grant us any favors."

"That's it exactly," I say. "I think maybe we hurt its feelings. When I said no, I picked up with my new powers a sort of... disappointment. Maybe even loneliness. The *talentum* has been locked away for so long, and all it wants is for its powers to be used and recognized. When it offered to make us all powerful beings, it was sorta like if someone made you an extra special cake and you told them, 'no, thanks, I don't like cake.'"

"That's crazy," Roar says and my stomach dips. I thought he would support me on this. But then he finishes, "Who doesn't like cake?"

I laugh. "That's exactly what I mean. It didn't understand where we were coming from."

"Let me get this straight. What you're saying is that magical objects have feelings too?" Helena sniffs.

"You're in love with a hundreds-of-years-old Casanova and horns sprout out of your head on occasion," I reply. "I think stranger things have happened than a magical object with resentment issues."

"She's right," Maddie agrees. "I think Crystal has good instincts."

After a moment, Helena nods. "Fair," she accepts, and coming from her that's a huge concession. "So what? We tell the *talentum* we're sorry?"

"Or we could offer to eat 'the cake.'" Maddie adds in a quieter voice.

Helena scoffs. "You think we should accept the all-powerful powers and leave our earthly selves behind in order to appease it?"

"I didn't say should. I said could," Maddie clarifies.

I bite my lip, uncertain, while on either side of me Harmony and Roar grab hold of each of my hands and squeeze them tight, as if trying to hold me here in my physical body. As if I need their encouragement! I am totally happy staying right where I am.

Harmony doesn't chime in, neither do any of the boys. They know that this is something we have to work out for ourselves.

"I think we just have to see," I say. "If all else fails, then yes, we may have to make that sacrifice."

"We wouldn't all have to; maybe just one of us?" Helena says, always problematic.

"And who should that be?" Maddie asks. "I have kids."

"I have a child too," Helena shoots back.

"My life isn't worth less because I don't have children," I say quietly. I just found love. Real love with Roar. Not the superficial based on lies relationship I had with Bobby.

"I didn't mean that," Maddie tells me, upset. Her eyes are wet and mine sting in response.

"I know, but it might not be enough," I say.

"It might want all of us now," Helena adds.

A little sob escapes Maddie and she presses her face into Aden's sleeve.

"We don't know if it will come to that," I say. "Maybe we can offer it something else it wants."

"Like what?" Helena asks doubtfully.

"We'll just have to ask it," I say, crossing my arms, determined.

"And what do *we* do?" Aden finally asks. "Kick dirt while we wait for you ladies to decide if you'll return to us?"

"You'll fight," I tell the guys. "I think we'll have to touch the *talentum* to talk with it. We'll need your help getting close and then keeping all of Busk's goons away."

"Got it," Roar says. "Women touch things, men punch things."

I pat his head, thankful for this man.

"Yes, babe," I tell him. "Go punch things."

26

———

Ford's magical tracker on Helena's piece of the *talentum* once again comes in handy, as we're able to use it to follow Busk's plane. We end up landing on an island somewhere in the ocean. We're in a chopper and it's not quiet, so Busk has to know we're right on his tail. But he's so convinced that he's going to be turned into a god in just a few moments, it doesn't really matter.

The guys pile out of the chopper, Aden already tossing a fireball from palm to palm, apparently recovered from the gas. Ford lifts up his shirt, revealing a holster with a gun already tucked inside. After checking the weapon, he reholsters it. Then he repeats this action with another gun on his ankle and a third tucked into the back of his pants.

"Wow, he's packing!" I say. Roar turns toward Ford with a threatening gleam in his eyes, and I quickly clarify, "With guns, he's got guns."

"Hmph, puny guns," Roar replies, satisfied.

"And brains," Ford adds. "Who was the guy doing all the research earlier?"

"Babe," Helena gives his shoulder a pat. "You're the world's best lover and a brilliant scholar."

Ford gives her one of his charm-packed smiles. "And..."

Clearly he wants her to add that he's an amazing fighter as well.

Instead she simply says, "Be careful."

He looks at Aden with his fireballs and Roar, stripping down so he can do his berserker thing. "I can throw a mean punch and I'm an excellent shot. You wouldn't be worried except that I'm standing between these two guys."

"Actually, your having those two guys at your back is why I'm not more worried."

Aden gives Ford a reassuring slap on the back...that sends the smaller man forward several steps. "He will be fine. We all will."

Helena's lips tighten, but she seems to know that this isn't her battle to fight. Not when she has her own. "Okay ladies, what's our move?"

"I'll check things out," Maddie says taking a deep breath. A gust of the wind lifts her up so she can have a birds-eye view of the island. Almost immediately she floats back down.

"Busk is setting up for his ritual," she tells us. "He's got enough loyal goons still with him that the guys are going to have their hands full."

At that comment, there's a sudden explosion. Aden has thrown a fireball, and a tree the size of our helicopter goes flying past us, aflame. A bloodthirsty scream follows that, then loud shouts and some gunfire.

"Sounds like our men are carrying out their end," Maddie says.

I give Helena's hand a reassuring squeeze, knowing she's worried about Ford. Even though Roar is an ancient super-soldier, I know how she feels, because I'm worried about him too. Busk is wily, and underestimating the harm he can cause has gotten us in trouble before.

"Alright." Maddie, always the mom, draws us into a circle. "I'm going to observe Busk, try to get a better idea of what's going on. How is everyone else feeling in terms of their powers? Are we all recovered from the gas?"

I know I am, because I just about wiped out Busk earlier. Helena closes her eyes and the earth moves under our feet.

"I don't know that I'm one hundred percent," she admits. "But I can fight."

"I feel the same," Maddie nods. "But it's time to go, no matter what."

The three of us share a long look, then nod. These are my sisters, not just my sister-wives. We're going into this together, and we'll come out together—or none of us will.

27

———————

Maddie calls on the breeze and hovers in the air just above the stand of trees we're hiding in. She puts her hand around the piece of hair braided with mine and Helena's, while Helena and I do the same. A moment later, it's like we're seeing through Maddie's eyes.

Busk is at the center of the field, dipping his hands into the guts of a dead man wearing a pilot's uniform. I can't imagine it's good for morale seeing how disposable Busk considers his workers, but I guess he's beyond such worries at the moment. His men—he seems to have an unlimited supply—are busy fighting with our guys anyway, and it looks like they've got their hands full.

Aden is ducking behind trees and taking potshots with fireballs, while Roar is full-on assaulting three guys at a time. Ford, meanwhile, seems to think this is a paintball match instead of a battle to the death. He's doing combat rolls to move between various cover and getting off shots where he can. I'm pretty sure I hear him yell, "Yippee Ki Yay Motherfucker."

He and Helena really are a perfect pair.

That happy thought bubble is popped rather rudely as we watch Busk through Maddie's eyes and see him pull a man's intestines from his body and drape them over his neck like a bloody necklace.

"Sick," I mutter, a hand over my mouth.

"Can you imagine the stink?" Helena adds aloud. "What a terrible choice."

Helena mutters something about how using balls for earrings would be way better—especially Busk's balls. I reach over and give her a comforting pat on the back.

Meanwhile, Maddie is still watching Busk. With his hands covered in gore, Busk reaches for the *talentum*.

Within a second she's back on the ground beside us. "Did you see? He's doing the ritual. We need to go—now!"

There's no time for argument or discussion. Maddie zips through the air as a geyser of dirt erupts underneath Helena, taking her to Busk. I call all the water around us, and it zips toward me. From the dew on trees to the humidity in the air, it boils around me, and I'm moved on a finger of water to follow in the path of my sisters. All three of us drop to the ground in front of Busk at the same time. He looks up, blood streaking his face.

"You're too late," he says, as he places the final piece—my ring, over the base and globe. "I'm about to become a god."

"You're about to become a bad memory," Maddie says. "Like night terrors for a toddler, but not as bad, because those you can't wake—"

"Fuck off, dickwad," Helena interrupts Maddie's soliloquy about parenting and hits him with a ball of dirt the size of an SUV. It knocks him sideways, the intestines looped around his neck flying through the air. They're caught by invisible fingers of wind that send them back toward Busk in ricochet, wrapping around his neck. He screams, fingers digging into them as he chokes.

Suddenly, there's a witch at his side, one that doesn't mind moral ambiguity and low pay, it seems. She hits Maddie with a counterattack, one that sends her spinning through the air, straight towards a tree. Helena's concentration is broken as she follows Maddie's path, her brow furrowing as she brings up a mound of soft dirt to catch our sister. The ground unfurls into a catcher's mitt and Maddie lands safely. Straightening her skirts and—dear god, really?—blushing as she realizes she flew right over Ford's head.

"Sorry!" she says, but he only smiles and calls back, "Nothing I haven't seen before!"

Busk's witch spins on me, but she's confused, unclear about whether to attack or not. And no wonder...I haven't done anything yet. After seeing who Busk is deep inside, a frightened child, I couldn't kill him. And now I'm not even sure if I can hurt him.

"Busk...Geoff," I say gently, as he pulls the intestines away from his neck. "Please, listen to me. I know you're scared. I know you're lonely. But if you could just—"

"Shut her the fuck up," Busk says, and the witch snaps her head at me. Suddenly, my teeth feel like they are soldered together. I literally can't open my mouth. But I don't need words to communicate with water.

Take her out, I think, and a huge hand of water emerges from the ocean, hovering over the two of them like a hand waiting to deliver judgment. I'm trembling, trying to keep it under control, not allowing it to fall and crush both Busk and the witch. She glances upward, goes pale, and looks over at Busk.

"Not worth it," she decides. "I'm out." She dashes off into the trees, but Helena gives the ground under the witch's feet a little buckling, sending her onto her hands and knees. From the look on her face, she wants to do more.

But she can't. She's tired.

Maddie, too, looks exhausted as she straightens her shoulders and locks eyes with me. She's ready to go back in, but are her powers? They were both exposed to the gas longer than I was, and clearly they are still affected. I toss my head and the water hand above us recedes back into the ocean, droplets of saltwater falling as Busk regains his feet, and moves back to the *talentum.*

"You stupid bitch," he sneers. "No, I don't want to talk about my feelings, or my childhood, or why I am the way I am. Don't you get it? I actually *like* being bad. I *like* hurting people, and I'm going to *love* being a god."

Maddie and Helena are back at my side, and we stare down Busk across the *talentum* as he slides the ring over the other two pieces, murmuring an incantation under his breath.

There's a rush of air, like a vacuum has opened, and then the *talentum* begins to glow.

"It's happening," Maddie says, the light from the *talentum* reflected in her eyes.

Busk and the *talentum* are limned in a circle of blinding light. I squint toward him, his brow furrowed in concentration. He seems to be locked in some sort of struggle. I hope this means that the *talentum* is seriously considering frying his ass for even daring to put his nasty hands on it. Or maybe it's just infusing him with the powers that it took the rest of us months to see.

Maddie comes to my side and Helena joins us. I grasp their hands. We move forward into the light and when the *talentum* is in front of us, we each reach forward. Our hands land on the part of the *talentum* we each consider our own. I touch the outer ring, Maddie the round globe center, and Helena the sunburst base.

Power surges through me, knocking my teeth together. Maddie gasps beside me and Helena lets loose a curse. It feels like a pressure is building in my body, and I'm about to blow apart.

I close my eyes and try to reach out to the *talentum*. There's a jolt and I barely keep my grip. I tighten my fingers and steel my resolve.

"Don't fight it!" I yell to Maddie and Helena.

We want to speak with you, I send mentally with everything I have. *Please, hear us.*

The pressure in my body eases suddenly. My eyes fly open to find that I'm in a space that reminds me a bit of the astral plane. But unlike the wispy white nothingness of that place, wherever I am now is big and blue and deep.

It's like being in the middle of the sky, among the stars. Maddie and Helena are at my side, and I only have to glance at their faces to see the wonder on them.

"It's amazing," Maddie says. "When people say awesome, this is what it truly means."

"Awe inspiring," I agree.

"Maybe it wouldn't be so bad to exist here for all eternity," Helena adds.

Maddie's face falls and I'm reminded of why we're here. We need to speak with the *talentum*. I search the expanse, so beautiful, except for a big ugly blot on the horizon—Busk.

"There!" I say and shoot toward him like a rocket. Maddie and Helena follow behind.

As we get nearer the dark blob comes into focus. It's definitely Busk.

"Hello ladies." He grins at us, like it's all over and he's won. "Nice of you to join me here."

"We're not here to see you," Helena informs him.

"Those intestines around your neck belong to someone's son," Maddie scolds, "Did you ever think of that?"

"No," Busk admits. "But now that I have, I have to say...it makes no difference to me at all."

I tune them out. Busk is a distraction. And Helena is right—he's not who we're here to see. Or maybe not see. To talk. To feel. And feeling is my gift. The one that the *talentum* gave to me.

I pull my power to me, close to my chest in a hug, and then release it out, searching for the *talentum*, for its center.

Child of the water, it says. *I did not expect to see you again. Our dealings were over.*

I look to Maddie and Helena. Both are wide eyed and staring into the far distance, letting me know that they're hearing the voice too.

"We also thought our dealings were over. But we realized that we were...selfish," I tell the *talentum*. "We took from you without ever asking what we could give back."

"What is this?" Busk demands, his voice intruding. It's as if he's not on this phone call but rather just nearby enough to catch snippets of it. "I am going to wield the *talentum's* power. I am giving all of myself to it."

"How could you possibly choose him?" Maddie cries out. "He's awful."

"He might literally be the last person on the planet," Helena adds.

Yes, the *talentum* agrees. *But is he not also single-minded? Focused. He wants me above all else.*

"Well, that sure explains why the *talentum* rejected Robert," Helena muses. "He could never stay focused on just one thing. Or woman."

"Shhh," I hush her. "Now is not the time."

The child of the earth is right, the *talentum* says. *That man wanted everything. Nothing would ever be enough.*

"And how is Busk different?" Maddie demands.

But I already know the answer to this. I have seen inside of him. I know exactly what he is made of.

"Power," I say. "Bobby wanted that too, but he also wanted love. I mean, look at us. And the kids too. He just needed so much love."

"Oh, Bert," Maddie says softly. And although Helena stays silent, she does give a little sigh.

Our husband was a flawed man, but unlike Busk he wasn't evil. I suppose that should be a small comfort. and he paid for his sins. It's strange, but I'm glad Bobby was a no good dirty-dog cheat. He's the one who brought us all together.

But this isn't about Bobby, I remind myself. The *talentum* had no trouble rejecting him. Now I need it to see why Busk should be rejected as well.

"Busk wants power," I tell the *talentum*, "and he *is* single-minded, but the source of his need is a smallness inside of him."

"Spoiler alert," Helena breaks in. "It's his dick."

I am about to shush her again when I sense a hint of... humor from the *talentum*. So the all-powerful magical object is a fan of dick humor. Who knew?

"Yes," I tell the *talentum*, "Busk was a short dick man, although he's had that problem magically fixed."

Suddenly, I can feel that Busk has been brought into the conversation.

Let the man defend himself...if he can, the *talentum* says.

"Defend myself?" Busk demands wildly. "From what?

"A smack of a ruler," Helena snarks. "A short one."

"What have these hysterical bitches been saying about me?" Busk yells, a bit hysterically.

"Crystal says you're a small man," Maddie clarifies. She holds out her pinky and wiggles it.

The child of the air is correct. These women have told me that you're too small to hold my power.

Busk puffs out his chest in a typical macho sort of way. "I've never had any complaints and I'm willing to demonstrate on all three of you."

"Ew," I say.

"No, thank you," Maddie answers more primly.

"Try it and you'll find out what it feels like to chew on your own dick." This last one is from Helena. Clearly.

"Look. Truly look," I say to the *talentum*, and then I reach out to Busk and spiritually pants him.

I don't show the *talentum* the size of his manhood, but the way its size has eaten away at him. There's a smallness inside of him, and it's made him a bully. The type of man who is cowardly at heart but talks big and uses others to take the real risks for him.

"He will never put himself on the line," I tell the *talentum*. "He will wield your power but never give back any of himself."

"*I see now what you mean*, the *talentum* replies. I can feel it bending our way.

I give Helena a poke, the signal that now she should speak up—and use her amazing lawyer negotiating skills.

"Make us the sole guardians of your power," Helena suggests. "We will work together to wield it for the greater good."

Your greater good? the *talentum* queries.

"No," Maddie says. "The world's. Odds are that Busk and his little weenie would eventually destroy the world and then your power would be good for nothing and no one. But we'll safeguard the world and its people and make sure that all know where our strength comes from. You."

I can feel the *talentum* likes what we're saying.

How do I know that the three of you will do as I say?

"We'll prove it," I say, looking to Maddie and Helena.

I show the *talentum* what is inside each of us the same way I did with Busk.

I display Maddie's nurturing essence, Helena's fierceness and belief in justice, and then my own...weakness. Except it's not weakness. I'm tenderhearted and want to believe the best of people. But that doesn't make me an idiot. It makes me someone who can see what the world could be if we all lived together in harmony.

I see, the *talentum* says. And I think it does. It focuses its attention on Busk. *Are you as they say, a bully and a coward?*

"Why would you even listen to these bitches?" Busk spits. "They didn't seek you out. I hunted your parts for years and didn't stop until they were mine. While they were just weak women who'd been fooled by their philandering husband. You gave them power because there were no other good options at the time. But now, you got me. I'm the one meant to rule. Me."

Busk is sweating at the end of this speech and there's more than a hint of desperation. And yet...the *talentum* doesn't fry him on the spot.

Instead, it says, *I have made my decision.*

A bright light surrounds us, and I reach for my sisters, grabbing each of their hands. And then I'm blinking in the bright sunlight of the day.

"We're alive," I say.

I look around. No Busk. And our boys have subdued the rest of his goons.

A breeze kicks up around us. "Maddie?" I ask.

"It's not me!" she says. "Look!"

A waterspout has appeared and is moving toward us. Behind Helena a tornado of dirt appears. The three cyclones —--one of air, one of water, one of dirt—surround us. I pull the girls into a group hug.

I have accepted your proposal, the *talentum* tells us. *But I have given you each one third of my power. You will work together to save the world.*

The wind, water, and dirt create a vortex in which we are lifted into the air. *Do you accept these conditions?*

"Yes!" we all shout as one.

We float back down as the *talentum* shakes and uncombines itself back into three pieces.

I stoop and pick up my ring. When I touch it, I feel the power that it gives me, but also the responsibility. I can also see into the aether. And I see Busk.

"What about him?" I ask.

This bargain that we've struck...has changed me, the *talentum* intones. *I know that you do not wish this man dead, despite all the harm he has done.*

"Well, maybe we can make an exception for him..." Helena starts.

"No!" I say. "But we can't just let him loose. He's petty and dangerous."

I shall make him impotent in his hatred. A bit of metal from each of the three pieces breaks off and floats together. With a golden glow it melts and grows, surrounding Busk. He shouts in alarm, but doesn't seem to be in any pain.

The metal encapsulates him, then shrinks into a tiny ball. With a metallic ring, it drops to the ground. *He is imprisoned. He can only leave when called upon to do good.*

"Who decides if he's good or not?" Maddie asks.

"We do," I answer, picking up the metal ball and giving it a shake.

"I think we should throw that ball into the ocean," Helena says, reaching down and picking up her part of the *talentum*.

"Maybe he can earn forgiveness," I say.

"So is he, like, a genie now?" Maddie asks.

"Please don't tell me we have to rub him..." Helena groans.

I think... "Busk," I whisper.

Busk appears, the metal bauble dangling around his neck. "I'm gonna kill every single one of you..." he starts. But he doesn't move.

"You can't," I tell him. "You have to do good things. From now on."

"We should make him give away all his money," Maddie suggests.

"And live the rest of his days like Mother Teresa," Helena agrees.

"Maybe we can just start with an apology?" I turn to Busk. "Well?"

He gulps. "If you think that I'm going to..."

I snap my fingers and he disappears into the metal ball. "Let's give him some time to think about it," I say.

"You know..." Helena starts, "We don't really need him to give away all his money. I can wear the magic appearance-changing necklace and pretend to be him."

I laugh. That's such a Helena idea. "Maybe let's talk about it tomorrow?" I say.

I see Roar and the boys waiting for us off to the side.

Right now, I want to go to the love of my life and give him a kiss that will create a tsunami.

And I do.

EPILOGUE
ONE YEAR LATER

shes to ashes. Dust to dust. Flesh to Hydra.

Everything is the same as that night two years ago.

By which I mean that nothing is the same...but we've gathered back at the wharf to remember our dearly departed husband and to once again feed the Hydra which is as close as we can get to Bobby's mortal remains.

Since we don't have a dead shared husband to give to the Hydra, we brought some hamburger meat. Helena wanted to do fancy steaks, but Maddie told her that ground beef was two for one this week and the sea monster wouldn't know the difference.

I had just wanted to throw flowers into the water for Bobby, but that idea was voted down.

So now we're tossing out handfuls of ground beef into the ocean and the water is starting to churn a little violently. It might be the Hydra, or it might be something else. This is

Jersey in the age of supernatural creatures, after all, so it's best to believe—and be prepared—for anything to happen.

Unlike that tense night, the three of us are laughing and joking. We went from strangers united by a terrible betrayal to sister-wives to...Goddesses for Hire.

Yeah, we opened a business to use our gifts for good. We only take on clients whose causes are worthy and we never charge them—although Maddie usually convinces the ones with money to donate to the *Talentum* Foundation. Which is going strong and helping rebuild the post-supernatural world. It should be; Busk gave all of his money to it.

Along with going public about our powers, we also brought the *talentum* out into the spotlight. There was no point in hiding it from treasure hunters anymore, we realized; the word was clearly out.

And we also thought the *talentum* would like the attention. It had been hidden away for too long. We put our heads together and decided that we could use our story to inspire women all over the world.

We started with local news—leaving Bobby's name out of it. The story spread on social media and got picked up by The Today Show. Then some producers with the Woman's Movie Channel came to us wanting to make a movie. We said okay.

It ended up being a trilogy, all of them set during Christmas and in a sweet seaside town that did not look like New Jersey (they filmed it in Vancouver). Still, the important stuff was there.

We found our power and also true love.

And then we lived happily ever after.

Although really, it's been more like busily ever after. 'Cause life has been bustling.

Oh! And the *talentum* is now merch.

Not the real one, of course.

But you can see replicas of the *talentum* in most gift shops—especially in the cheesy tourist traps on the Shore. And we sell very pretty ones on our own website. All proceeds from the sale go to the Goons Reformation Society. That's not what it's officially called, of course; Helena gave it some long-winded lawyery-sounding thing. But really it's to help guys like Frank who end up working for bad guys and don't know how to get out.

"You ladies done out there?" Aden calls from the parking lot where we told the men to wait. Revisiting Bobby's final eating—er, resting—place was something we had to do alone.

But now it feels good to call back, "Yes! And please bring us some wet-wipes—our hands are full of raw meat."

I hear the rumble of Ford's voice and then Aden and Roar's answering laughter, telling me he probably turned my innocent comment about raw meat into something dirty.

Beside me Helena is giggling too. Yes, honest to goodness giggling. Of all of us, sometimes I think she's changed the most.

But then again, Maddie is totally different too. How else to explain her saying, "Oh forget the wet wipes. Crystal, just send some water over here for us to splash our hands in."

I do, pulling from the ocean and creating a little pool floating in mid-air. We scrub our hands in the water and then Maddie pulls a small bottle of hand sanitizer from her pocket. Which just goes to show that there are ways a person changes, and ways they stay the same.

As for me...I don't know if I've changed that much. I still live with my mother, although Roar and I built a tiny house out back for a little privacy. I'm still a dreamer more than a fighter and I probably always will be.

I guess, when I think about it, none of us really changed from who we were. We really just became the truest and best versions of ourselves.

"Skinny dipping!" Roar cries, running down the beach stark naked.

"No!" I cry out, thinking of the churning water.

But it's no use. Roar swings me up into the arms and then heads straight into the rolling waves.

Laughing, I decide to give into the moment. I pull my dress off over my head and fling it into the water.

Carry that to shore for me, please, I say to it. *And please make sure all the hungry beasties keep away from us.*

The water burbles back at me, happy to do my bidding.

"Come on!" I yell to the others. "The water's great!"

And then just in case they were thinking of holding back, I send a huge rogue wave their way and soak them.

That pretty much settles it.

The sun sets on us, not riding off into the sunset, but instead frolicking in the waves off the Jersey Shore. I'm sure anyone seeing us would think that we should be old enough to know better. A bunch of middle-aged fools. But if they looked closer, they'd see us for what we really are:

A gorgeous, cursed Casanova, a perfectly sculpted Viking berserker, an irresistibly hot (in more ways than one) demi-god from Hades, and three women powerful enough to love and be loved by them.

Grave New World is the first book in an all new paranormal mystery series filled with laughs and romance!

———

Supes were once just a myth. That's where Edie's story starts. But by the end of it...she'll have changed the whole world.

Read Fire & Flood: Mythverse Book 1 ebook for FREE! You can find it wherever books are sold!

At Mount Olympus Academy, a little learning is a dangerous thing...

Revenge. That's why I decided to join the assassination class at Mount Olympus Academy. A monster killed my father and grandmother - and I'm going to make them pay.

But first I have to learn how.

I'm Edie. Once I was just a normal girl with asthma and a bad back. Now, though, I'm at a school taught by Greek gods. My classmates are vampires, witches, and shifters. We're all training to fight in the war between the gods and monsters.

There's also...Val. He's a vampire, but he's different from the others. Plus, he's got secrets too.

I get secrets. The wings that sprout from my back were hidden from me my entire life. I also sometimes breathe fire. But no one - including me - can figure out what I fully shift into. Honestly...a part of me doesn't want to know.

But if I'm going to avenge my family, I need to figure it out before I flunk out.

Read the Fire & Flood ebook for FREE! You can find it wherever books are sold!

FIRE & FLOOD SNEAK PEEK

Chapter 1

My parents and sister are at the airport, getting ready to board a plane headed toward Greece. Meanwhile, I'm waiting to be checked out of the hospital.

I'm supposed to be on that flight with them—a three-month work trip that my archeologist mom organized. But two weeks earlier I came down with a virus that turned into pneumonia. This, combined with my lifelong mortal enemy, asthma, made breathing suddenly a lot harder. And then nearly impossible.

That's where the hospital comes in.

The doctors saved my life. And then totally ruined it by telling my parents I should stay home tucked under a blanket on my grandmother's couch so I could be all rested up for my senior year of high school come fall.

I honestly didn't think they would really go without me. No offense to my grandma, but she's pretty old and kinda wobbly. No way would my parents leave their sickly daughter with her while they were on a totally different continent.

"Leave me behind? Screw that," I'd laughed right after the doctor who gave me the bad news left the room.

No one else laughed. Mom, Dad, and my older sister Mavis just stared back at me.

I swallowed, not liking those looks. "Right?"

"Well, sweetheart—" Mom paused as she took off her glasses and began to clean them on the hem of her shirt. It's one of her favorite avoidance tactics. When I was ten and asked her what sex was, she polished so long and hard that she snapped them in half.

Suddenly I was worried.

"Dad?" I turned to my no-bullshit go-to guy.

"Sweetheart, we rented out our house. Not to mention that for Mom, it's a work trip."

"And I'm getting college credits for an internship," Mavis added. That one really stung. Mavis and I have always been close. Sure there's the usual sisterly bickering, but beneath that we genuinely like each other. I was looking forward to spending the summer together exploring Greece with her and hearing about her first year of college out in California. All year she only came home for Christmas and I missed her like crazy. But now she's heading off again. Without me.

I argued—eloquently, I believe, or as eloquently as someone who has to suck on an inhaler when they get too worked up —for my right to go on this trip. Sure, it was about having fun, but it was also about education, and opportunity and... and the fact that I'd already rubbed it in all my ex-friends' faces that I was going.

In the end, we compromised. And by compromised I mean they just decided.

They would go to Greece as planned.

I would stay with Grandma and she would teach me how to knit. Which was also, Mom pointed out, a learning opportunity. They presented me with a big cotton bag filled with a rainbow's worth of yarn and my very own pair of knitting needles.

It was one hell of a consolation prize. But I wasn't raised to be a sore loser, so I forced a smile and a thank you. Somehow I even managed to wish them well on their travels. Did an evil voice deep inside wish them months of chronic diarrhea? Maybe. But at least I didn't say it aloud.

Maybe I can knit them some diapers.

Now, I hold my bag of knitting supplies as a nurse wheels me out to the curb where my grandma waits behind the wheel of her '85 Lincoln. As I settle myself in the passenger seat my phone bings with a text.

MAVIS: We just boarded.

MAVIS: Didn't get seats together, but luckily I've already made friends.

A pic follows this second text. Mavis and some unbelievably good-looking guy grinning into the camera.

That is so typical Mavis. Even her bad luck turns out good. Stuck by herself and ends up next to one of the hottest guys in the universe.

The car jerks sideways and thumps up onto the curb and then down again. My phone flies out of my hand.

"Almost got that sonofabitch!" Grandma yells, giving her steering wheel a slap that I can't decide is meant to be congratulatory or an admonishment. I look back to see an alligator sunning himself beside the ditch at the side of the road. Gran hates them ever since they ate her Bichon Frise, Elsa, and attempts to mow them down with her car whenever possible. "Next time, next time," she mutters.

"Hey Grandma," I say, in my best poor pathetic left behind tone of voice. "Maybe I can drive the rest of the way home? Get some practice in? It would really lift my spirits."

Grandma shoots me a look that is clearly meant to convey she may be seventy-three, but she ain't senile yet. "Sweetheart, you've failed that driving test what is it...eight times now? Didn't the last tester beg you to quit before you killed someone?"

"Grandma, I know how to drive," I protest. "I'm just a bad test taker."

I'm actually epically terrible. I tend to freeze up in high stress situations. And there is no situation more stressful than trying to go where you want without having to beg Mom or Dad for a lift.

"You're sick, Edie. What kind of grandma do you think I am? Why not rest a little bit on the way home? You look a little peaked." The light changes and Grandma floors it, slamming me back into my seat.

Another battle lost. It's true, though, I am tired. I close my eyes and try to pretend I'm on a plane. It's lifting up into the sky, to travel across an ocean, before finally settling down in the land where gods were born.

———

As we pull into the parking lot behind Grandma's condo the typical Florida afternoon downpour begins. Grandma slowly totters along while holding her little old lady umbrella that she always keeps in her handbag over my head so I don't get soaked and end up back in the hospital. It's nice and all, but I'm about three feet taller than Grandma so I end up just kind of walking hunched over to get under the umbrella, which doesn't make my chest feel too hot.

Finally we get into the creaky old elevator. It grumbles and lurches its way up to the sixth floor. By the time Grandma unlocks the door all I want to do is cry.

"What's that face for?" Dad asks.

I gasp. He's seated at Grandma's breakfast bar with a cup of coffee. Not on a plane to Greece—but here.

"You stayed!" I rush forward, throwing my arms around him. "I knew you wouldn't leave without me. Where are Mom and Mavis? Are they mad they missed their trip?"

The look on Dad's face as he peels away from me tells me everything I need to know. "Edie, it was Mom's grant. And her dream. You know that. Asking her to miss this chance..."

I swallow hard. Force a nod. "Right. I know."

And I do know. Mom met Dad when they were both studying abroad in Greece years ago. They fell in love, she got pregnant, and Mom decided to stay home with us kids and give up her career until we were older. I never really understood it. Why couldn't she do both?

When I ask Mom she'll only says she was overly worried about our safety just like any young mom. Really, though, Dad's always been the more overprotective one, while Mom is constantly pushing me to let go and embrace my wild side. I've tried to tell her I don't have a wild side, that I'm pretty sure I was born without one. That's when she gets this glint in her eye and insists that someday I'm going to surprise myself. If Mavis is around she always like to add, "In bed." Ha ha ha, Mavis.

Anyway, once I started high school, Mom decided it was time to pick up where she left off. She finished her degree and then this opportunity to work in Greece came up. Dad didn't like it. They tried to hide the fact they were arguing, but even though neither of them are screamers, there's always a certain tone to their voices when they're upset. Eventually Mom won and well, it was immediately obvious how excited she was. Suddenly Greece this and Greece that was all Mom could talk about.

So yeah, unless I was on my deathbed, there's no way Mom wasn't getting on that airplane. And Mavis, well, she was always Mom's favorite, while I've always been Dad's.

I hug Dad again. "Thank you for coming back for me."

He ruffles my hair. Or tries. It's wet, so he just sort of rubs my head instead. "Well, I had to decide who needed more help staying out of trouble—you or your mom. You won, but only just barely."

"Hey, Dad," I smile up at him. "Speaking of trouble...since we're here all summer with nothing to do, maybe you can help me get more driving practice in."

"Aw, baby girl." Dad smiles fondly. "I would rather spend an afternoon wrestling alligators than be inside a vehicle you're driving."

"Dad!"

"But I did have an idea." He rummages in his pocket and then holds up two laminated cards with a ta-da expression.

"Those are bus passes."

"Yup. Good all summer. I figured, well, maybe we could explore the public transportation system in our fair city. It's eco-friendly and it'll be an adventure!"

I stare at Dad. He is working so hard to sell this. Only the vice principal of a junior high school would be this excited about bus passes, and only a monster would burst his bubble.

"Wow. Bus passes and knitting. Best summer ever." Somehow I manage to keep most of the sarcasm out of my voice.

Dad grins back at me. "Best summer ever," he echoes.

Thing is, I think he means it.

———

Read the rest of the Fire & Flood ebook for FREE! You can find it wherever books are sold!

Chapter 1

Cleaning up after a vampire rave sucks.

Pun intended.

My first one, I came armed with a whole truckload of hydrogen peroxide, expecting blood stains everywhere. In my mind, they covered the walls and floors and ceilings. I expected something like what a plasma donation center would look like if it was run by someone hopped up on way too much Mountain Dew.

It turns out, though, that vampires are not messy eaters. You might even say they don't like to waste a single drop of their meal. It's sacred to them the way Ho-Ho's were to my seventh-grade math teacher.

So yeah, it's not the prospect of scrubbing away blood stains that's getting me down as I drive through the warehouse district searching each building for the 6669 the vamps paint on the wall of their chosen party spot. The number's some sort of vampire humor, I think. Or maybe not. They're hard to read and I'm not interested in getting close enough to find out anything about them beyond that they pay in cash.

"Where is this stupid place?" I ask aloud, even though there's no one else in the van with me. Although...my van is kind of sentient. Like a cross between Christine and Herbie, it's both terrifying and adorable.

Vanna was stolen ages ago. Back when she...er, *it*, was just a normal Grand Caravan with stained seats and a dented back fender from some tailgating asshole. I figured that was the last I'd see of it, but a few months back I opened my door and there was Vanna (yes, I named her and yes I hate myself for it). The same...but also totally different.

I would've sent her straight back to the impound lot where she was found if it wasn't for the fact that I was desperate for transportation. The transmission had just died on my previous van and without wheels I had no job. So I used Vanna, figuring I could just pretend she was normal. Just another vehicle.

That didn't last long.

In response to my question, Vanna takes over steering, which is always annoying. But I forgive her as she parks us in front of a building, the 6669 on the wall straight ahead.

From the outside the warehouse looks totally unremarkable. Just another big boxy building. I can't hold back a big sigh as I grasp the handles on the giant sliding door. Putting all my weight into it, I pull the door hard. With a groan it gives way, gliding open and allowing a bright shaft of sunlight to cut through the dark interior.

"Aw fuck," I say as a giant water tank fills my vision. I'm not talking about some little pet store thing; this is Sea World size. I have no idea how I'm gonna drain this thing and scrub it spotless. That's the job, though. I'm supposed to leave only the dust motes and a sparkling clean tank behind when I'm done.

This alone would be a monumental task, but as I walk into the warehouse and closer to the tank and the moving shadows within, I know it's gonna get worse.

And it does.

Sharks. Big ones, too. They glide through the water with silent menace.

Those asshole vamps decided to have an underwater rave and feed on fucking sharks.

I thought the lions were the worst. Before that, I thought the pigs were the worst.

Clearly, I was wrong all those times. Because really, vampires are the worst. Always and forever—they are The. Worst.

I take a minute to swear viciously and creatively, cursing not just vampires but all the paranormal creatures that decided to come out of hiding a decade ago and totally screw up everything. Sometimes I hear people say that it's better to know than to live in ignorance. I disagree. The time when I believed that werewolves, harpies, and faeries were all just stories was a great time. An easier, simpler one too.

I was only in my early twenties when everything changed. My dad's cleaning business was struggling and I'd just graduated with a degree in English that I was quickly realizing was pretty much useless in the real world. Then we had a little apocalypse. Cities disappeared beneath the sea. Crops failed. And all the supes came out to play. Suddenly college degrees didn't mean much. Survival was our entire focus.

I got married to my boyfriend, 'cause it felt like we might all die and I guess I wanted to wear a white dress first? I don't know. It wasn't the greatest decision. I also went into business with Dad. But we revamped it. Pun intended.

Harper Cleaning became Down & Dirty: Supernatural Cleaning Services. Dad said we were kinda like the clean-up crew for the Ghostbusters. "Think about it," he'd say. "Someone had to mop up that marshmallow mess, and I bet they got paid good money. Hazard pay, right?"

He was right. The business thrived. My marriage failed. But overall, life was good.

Until my parents disappeared along with a few hundred thousand other folks.

But that's another story.

Right now, I gotta figure out how to get these sharks outta this tank.

Luckily, we're in the Newark Port district. I understand now why they chose this location. But still, the Bay is a good ten minutes away. Can a shark survive that long out of water?

Pulling out my phone, I start to Google.

Some people might think I'm just a cleaning lady, but in truth, this job requires way more than just a mop and broom.

Yesterday I was choking on feathers cleaning out a frat house that had been full of chicken shifter strippers. Today I'm wrestling sharks. Tomorrow I might be scrubbing harpy droppings off some vocal Humans First protester's roof and lawn.

Down & Dirty is more than just a job. It's a lifestyle.

Finish Grave New World and Read the whole 7 book series today!

ABOUT THE AUTHORS

DEMITRIA LUNETTA is the author of the YA books THE FADE, BAD BLOOD, and the sci-fi duology, IN THE AFTER and IN THE END. She is also an editor and contributing author for the YA anthology, AMONG THE SHADOWS: 13 STORIES OF DARKNESS & LIGHT. Find her at www.demitrialunetta.com for news on upcoming projects and releases.

KATE KARYUS QUINN is an avid reader and menthol chapstick addict with a BFA in theater and an MFA in film and television production. She lives in Buffalo, New York with her husband, three children, and one enormous dog. She has three young adult novels published with HarperTeen: ANOTHER LITTLE PIECE, (DON'T YOU) FORGET ABOUT ME, AND DOWN WITH THE SHINE. She also recently released her first adult novel, THE SHOW MUST GO ON, a romantic comedy. Find out more at www.katekaryusquinn.com

MARLEY LYNN is a lost child of the gods, who waits on the shores of Lake Erie for her parents to bring her home. In the meantime, she contents herself with reading, writing, and gardening. Find out more at www.MarleyLynn.com

ACKNOWLEDGMENTS

Thank you to Marin McGinnis for taking care of our copy edits!

And, of course, a big thank you to our families for putting up with us crazy writers.